Dear Romance Reader,

Welcome to a world of breathtaking passion and never-ending romance.
Welcome to *Precious Gem Romances*.

It is our pleasure to present *Precious Gem Romances*, a wonderful new line of romance books by some of America's best-loved authors. Let these thrilling historical and contemporary romances sweep you away to far-off times and places in stories that will dazzle your senses and melt your heart.

Sparkling with joy, laughter, and love, each *Precious Gem Romance* glows with all the passion and excitement you expect from the very best in romance. Offered at a great affordable price, these books are an irresistible value—and an essential addition to your romance collection. Tender love stories you will want to read again and again, *Precious Gem Romances* are books you will treasure forever.

Look for eight fabulous new *Precious Gem Romances* each month—available only at Wal★Mart.

Lynn Brown, Publisher

BEGINNER'S LUCK

Patricia Lynn

Zebra Books
Kensington Publishing Corp.

http://www.zebrabooks.com

ZEBRA BOOKS are published by

Kensington Publishing Corp.
850 Third Avenue
New York, NY 10022

Zebra and the Z logo Reg. U.S. Pat. & TM Off.

First Printing: September, 1997
10 9 8 7 6 5 4 3 2 1

Printed in the United States of America

Chapter One

Justin Holmes recognized trouble when he saw it. And the shapely brunette climbing out of her dark blue sports car was definitely trouble—spelled in all caps and bolded. She crossed the gravel parking lot with an easy, natural grace that shouted self-assurance. Wearing a loose, long-sleeved white shirt tucked into the narrow waist of tailored black slacks, she looked sensational.

And totally out of place against the rustic backdrop of Dale Hollow Lake.

It annoyed him that he couldn't define exactly why he felt so apprehensive about spending the next ten days with Ashley Harper. There was just something about the whole situation that set his nerves on edge.

With a resigned sigh, he adjusted his battered Met's baseball cap before starting down the stone steps of the Starlight Marina. The sooner these ten days started, the sooner they'd be over, he reasoned. All he had to do was his job. She'd learn all she needed to know, then be on her way. No problem.

As he approached, her pace slowed. Because of her sunglasses, he couldn't see her eyes, but knew her attention was focused on him.

"Miss Harper?" He asked just to be absolutely certain he had the right woman.

"Yes."

Stopping before her, he extended his hand. "Hello. I'm Justin Holmes."

"Mr. Holmes." She accepted his hand with a firm handshake. "It's nice to meet you."

Just as he'd expected, her skin was soft, her long nails perfectly manicured. He could easily picture her holding a delicate china teacup. Visualizing her handling a slimy, squirming fish was beyond his imagination.

"You had a nice day to drive up from Knoxville," he remarked.

"Yes, it's lovely. I hope the weather stays this nice the whole time I'm here."

Her voice intrigued him. The rich, smooth tone combined with her native Southern drawl produced an oddly seductive sound. Visions of steamy summer nights and long, slow kisses drifted across his mind.

Realizing he must be staring, he forced his bizarre thoughts back in line. "Well, according to the weather forecast for this area, it should be nice at least through Wednesday. After that it's a toss-up."

"We'll just have to do as much as we can by Wednesday." She hesitated. "Should I get my things?"

"Sure."

She turned and together they retraced her steps to her car. He watched as she opened the small trunk, revealing two large suitcases and one cosmetic case. She then walked around to open the passenger side of the car. When she returned, she had two large leather bags slung over her shoulder, her purse tucked under her arm, and a huge boom box complete with two tape decks in her hand.

"All ready," she stated.

He looked at her, then down at the luggage still in the trunk. She had to be kidding.

"Is something wrong?" Her inquiry was cool, controlled.

He felt the muscles in the back of his neck tense. Yes, it was definitely going to be a very long ten days. "Did you pack your whole closet?"

A strained silence stretched between them. "Pardon me?"

The iciness of her voice was definitely chilling, but he decided she might as well learn now that it was wasted on him. "Let me put it another way. Do you have anything in these cases that's appropriate for how we're going to spend the next ten days?" He intentionally let his gaze rake her from head to toe before inquiring with raised eyebrows, "Or are you planning to dress like that the whole time?"

He saw her shoulders stiffen as she drew in a sharp breath. Behind the dark glasses, her eyes never wavered from his. "Mr. Holmes, do you plan on being this arrogant the whole time we're together?"

He smiled slightly and crossed his arms against his chest. "Miss Harper, I doubt that I'll change my personality just to suit you."

They stared at one another a long, tense moment, each measuring the other. Justin felt something foreign and dangerous crackle in the air between them. He nearly shivered, feeling as if someone had just run a slow finger down the center of his back. The sharply charged atmosphere was unexpected and unnerving. He considered himself a damn good poker player, and was reasonably certain his unease didn't show as he continued to hold her gaze. But he couldn't deny being relieved when she finally broke the stalemate.

She shifted the heavy bags on her shoulder. "There's no need for you to worry about my wardrobe," she pointed out with stilted politeness. "If it's not suitable, then it's my problem. I won't hold you responsible for my obvious stupidity."

The sarcasm edging her voice further nudged his temper. He couldn't remember the last time he'd been this irritated by anything or anyone. Less than fifteen minutes in this woman's presence and his blood pressure was on the rise. Why she sparked this response in him wasn't an issue he cared to explore.

Common sense told him the safest thing to do was leave her and her luggage right where they were and go back to his cabin and his peaceful existence alone. He didn't need her money, and God knew he could do without the headache she promised to give him. She was a challenge he had no desire to take on.

A dozen reasons to turn and walk away came to mind. He could think of only one to finish what had been started. He owed Nick—plain and simple.

Justin hefted the two suitcases from the trunk and nearly groaned out loud. He wasn't a weakling by any stretch of the imagination, but whatever she'd packed weighed a ton.

Without further comment, he turned and started for his Blazer. He hoped Ashley Harper was smart enough to follow, because he didn't think he could speak without sounding winded.

Ashley stood in the middle of the sparsely furnished cabin and found her accommodations satisfactory.

A sleeper sofa took up one wall of the living room, a row of bookshelves filled another. A square wooden table with four ladder-back chairs, three of which matched, sat in the middle of the opening between the kitchen and the living room. The kitchen came equipped with a refrigerator and gas stove, plus all cooking and eating utensils.

A small bedroom boasted a full-size metal bed and a large chest of drawers made of pine. The bathroom was tiny, with a shower barely big enough to turn around in.

Far from fancy, the cabin was clean and did possess the two things she determined to be most essential—electricity and indoor plumbing. Learning to fish was one thing. Roughing it for ten days was another. She had no desire to commune too closely with nature.

She'd have to ask Justin where she could pick up some groceries. The mere thought of asking that man anything set off a spark of resentment. She'd already pegged him as a typical macho male. The domineering type who believed, no doubt, that a woman belonged either in the bedroom or the kitchen.

Ashley wondered how her father had come up with Justin to teach her to fish. She'd assumed he would send her to someone closer to his own age. Justin Holmes was clearly a generation younger than her father. The thought of spending ten days with him set off a ripple of unease that only annoyed her more. She'd be damned if she'd let some backwoods hillbilly intimidate her.

"He's just a conceited male chauvinist," she muttered as she used both hands to half-carry, half-drag one of her suitcases toward the bedroom.

She'd already decided Justin wasn't from the south. No way. He didn't possess the slow, Southern drawl or the laid-back attitude she'd expected. There was an edge to him, an inbred restlessness. He moved a little too quickly, spoke a little too sharply. And though it had faded some with time, his voice still held the hint of an Eastern accent. Justin Holmes was an East Coast Yankee, no doubt about it. She wondered how he'd ended up in these Tennessee hills.

Impatiently she pushed that thought away. She didn't care what had brought him here, and she wasn't about to let him ruin her stay.

She'd been looking forward to this trip for weeks. Learning new things always excited her. Learning new things that she could share with someone special was even better. True, her soon-to-be-fiancé hadn't been thrilled when she'd told him she was going to be away for ten days, but he'd forgive her soon enough when he discovered where she'd gone and why.

Although he didn't know it yet, Ashley planned to marry Geoffrey Anderson. They'd been seeing one another for six months, and he met just about all her criteria for the perfect mate. He was handsome, intelligent, and a gentleman. She felt content with him. They'd settle down into a nice, comfortable routine and live the rest of their lives together doing all the things they enjoyed. Like fishing.

When she'd heard Geoffrey mention to a friend that he liked to fish, Ashley had gone to her father, an avid angler himself, and asked him to hook her up with someone who could teach her to fish. That's how she came to be at Dale Hollow Lake with Justin Holmes. Enduring his annoying presence the next ten days wouldn't be the most fun she'd ever had, but she could handle it. She only hoped his fishing skills were sharper than his personality.

She went back for the other case and paused long enough to plug in her boom box and pop in a tape. A jumpy country beat pulsed out of the speakers. She cranked up the volume before returning to the bedroom to unpack.

Justin sat on the top step of his porch and absently stroked Dudley behind one floppy ear. The mutt's tail began a steady thump as he gazed up at his master with adoring black eyes.

Justin decided it was a good thing he liked country music. For the past hour a steady stream of Garth Brooks had been wafting on the late afternoon air, its source the cabin next door. He supposed he should be thankful Ashley Harper wasn't a heavy metal fan.

He glanced at his watch before pushing to his feet. Dudley rose too, ready to follow. Justin had affectionately dubbed him "The Shadow." After finding him abandoned at the end of the lane, weak and half-drowned from a summer thunderstorm, Justin had nursed him back to health. He tried to determine exactly what breed the dog might be, but never did figure it out. Dudley was a mid-sized mutt with thick black fur, a gentle nature, and a deep devotion to the man who had saved his life.

Man and dog followed the gravel drive cutting through the thick trees to the neighboring cabin Justin had built three years ago. He was thinking about building another. His reputation as a fishing guide had grown over the years, bringing him a steady stream of business. He'd discovered not all his clients wanted to spend their time on a houseboat on the lake or in a cabin at one of the area marinas. His cabin offered comfortable surroundings and privacy, an alternative many folks preferred.

As he climbed the steps to the porch, he could see through the screen door. Ashley wasn't anywhere in sight. He knocked, but knew the blaring music would cover the sound. He finally jerked the door open and stepped into the kitchen, Dudley right on his heels.

Justin took a moment to study the boom box and its many knobs and buttons. Figuring it would be easier to find Ashley in the small cabin than to determine which button controlled the sound of the machine, he started across the room.

He found her in the bedroom. She had her back to the door as she hung something in the closet. Standing in the doorway, he took a moment to admire the view. Her hips swayed gently in time with the music. The slacks she wore were by no means tight, but they hinted nicely at the curves beneath the fabric.

Deciding he'd better make his presence known, he started to speak at precisely the same moment she turned from the closet. The startled scream she emitted had Dudley scurrying for cover. Justin could only stand rooted to the spot as she brought a hand to her chest and closed her eyes.

"I knocked," he offered defensively.

When her eyes flew open, he expected sparks to fly from the dark depths and fry him alive.

"You knocked?" she shouted. "Did I answer?"

"No. But your music is so loud—"

He had the good sense to step back as she started toward him. She rushed past and went to the tape player. Her hand shot forward to punch one button. Sudden silence descended as she whirled to face him.

"There," she snapped. "Did it occur to you to just shut the thing off? Wouldn't that have made more sense?"

"I looked at it." He shrugged. "There are enough buttons and switches there to serve as command central for a SCUD missile launch."

"The one marked on/off might have been a good guess, don't you think?" She crossed her arms. "You nearly scared me to death."

"I'm sorry," he conceded grudgingly.

"Did you consider just pulling the plug? That would have worked."

He took a deep breath, feeling the first spark of temper. "Have you considered playing it at a more acceptable level of volume? Then maybe you'd hear the next time someone knocks."

"I won't have you skulking around here."

The spark of anger became a flame. It appeared she had a natural knack for pushing him to the limit in record time. "I wasn't skulking. I've already apologized. Take it or leave it."

She stared at him a long moment. "What did you want?"

"I wanted to know if you'd like to go into town and pick up some supplies."

"Yes, I need to do that. I'll be ready to go in a few minutes."

Hearing the dismissal in her voice, he inclined his head slightly and started for the door. He'd just pushed it open when she called out to him. He paused to look over his shoulder to see her standing in the doorway to the bedroom, her back to him.

"Could you tell me what this thing is under my bed?"

He walked back to her and peered into the room. She pointed toward the foot of the bed. Dudley had taken refuge there and now just his black nose poked out from under the blue bedspread.

"That's Dudley. You scared him when you screamed."

Justin looked over at her and found her eyes, a rich, chocolate brown, shooting sparks again. She stood close— close enough that he could detect the subtle scent of her perfume. It reminded him of sunshine and wildflowers. She was taller than he'd first thought, only a few inches shorter than his six feet. Strands of dark brown hair had worked themselves free from her casual ponytail to frame her face. There wasn't even a dusting of freckles across her pert nose to mar her smooth ivory complexion. He made a mental note to remember to make sure she wore a hat to protect her skin from the sun while they were fishing. She didn't offer him a smile, but her full lips parted slightly, and suddenly, all he could think about was testing their softness beneath his own.

"What is a Dudley?" she asked, her voice sounding slightly unsteady.

He wondered if he'd caused that. He thought about

touching his fingers to her throat, wondered if he'd find her pulse racing.

He wondered if he'd taken leave of his senses.

Forcing his attention away from her, he turned back to the dog. "Come on out, Dudley. Ashley won't scream at you again."

"I didn't scream at him. I was screaming at you."

"But you scared him." Justin crouched down and reached his hand toward the hesitant pooch. "Come on, boy. It's okay."

The bedspread shifted, and the dog hesitantly emerged. "There you go." Justin scratched him behind the ear before standing.

"He doesn't look like any dog I've ever seen before," Ashley said.

"Of course he doesn't. He's unique." Justin looked down at the dog. "Say hello to Miss Harper, Dudley."

Obediently, Dudley sat and lifted his paw.

"Oh," she said softly. Bending, she took the offered paw in her hand. "So you're a smart guy."

Her warm response surprised Justin. He figured the dog was beneath his prissy guest. But she knelt and stroked a hand along the thick fur. Dudley's tail began to pound forcefully against the wood floor, and Ashley laughed.

The husky sound drifted up to Justin, causing a strange sensation to skitter along his central nervous system. Simultaneously, a faint warning bell went off inside his head.

Still smiling, Ashley straightened. "He's so ugly, he's cute," she said, casting a quick glance to Justin.

He wasn't prepared. That one unguarded smile nearly knocked him off his feet. It softened her features and lit her eyes, a complete and totally unexpected transformation. He stared at her, unable to help himself. The single warning bell was joined by others, creating a symphony of alarm and reinforcing his first impression of trouble.

He pulled his gaze from hers and reached a hand down to Dudley. "Come on, Dud, let's go. Let me know when you're ready," he called to Ashley as he made a bee-line for the door.

Justin shook his head as he emerged into the sweet

spring air. A thick fog seemed to have encased his brain, seriously impairing his ability to think clearly. Pretty, pampered city girls were not a novelty to him. He'd grown up surrounded by them, had come to understand them early on. For the most part they were selfish and self-centered, and he'd decided a long time ago he wanted nothing to do with them.

So why did Ashley Harper make him feel like a teenager experiencing his first crush? She was everything he disliked in a woman. Yet, he couldn't deny the attraction that sparked so easily between them.

Had she felt it, too? He remembered the breathlessness of her voice and the awareness that had entered her eyes as he'd stood so close to her. Maybe it was just basic sexual attraction. He felt relief ripple through him. Sexual attraction he could handle. Either you did something about it, or you ignored it until it disappeared.

Well, he wasn't about to do anything about Ashley Harper. First of all, meaningless affairs were not his style. Second, his friendship with Nick Harper, Ashley's father, was too important to jeopardize. So that only left one alternative. Ignore the attraction for ten days and then she'd be gone. It was that simple.

The little town of Windsong sat protectively nestled in the bosom of rolling, tree-dense Tennessee hills. The city boasted a population of just over two-thousand. The fact that several of those folks lived deep in the hills and weren't seen more than once or twice a year, didn't keep them from being counted in the census.

The mayor considered Windsong a thriving community. Just last year a fast-food chain had built one of its restaurants on the edge of town close to the highway. That, combined with Peabody's Grocery, the Woodland Drive-In Theater, and the Dollar General made Windsong, in his expert opinion, a small town with plenty to offer.

Ashley climbed out of Justin's Blazer at Peabody's Grocery, immediately enchanted by the picturesque town. The town square, featuring a two-story red brick courthouse, was just down the street. The belfry clock chimed the hour, while a few old men dressed in faded denim overalls sat on park benches and watched patiently as the world drifted by. People were about, but no one seemed to be in much of a hurry. Traffic meandered down the main stretch, paused at the one stop light when necessary, and then continued on around the square.

A building on a distant overlook caught Ashley's attention, and she shaded her eyes as she looked up at it. "What's that?" she asked Justin as he came to stand beside her.

"That's the Cliffside Motel. It's used mostly by locals."

She dropped her hand and turned to look at him. "Pardon?"

"Every small town has a local motel. You know, a little love nest tucked away at the edge of town. In Windsong it just happens to sit on the highest point." He shook his head. "Seems like poor planning to me."

She arched a brow. "Do you use it often?"

"All the time."

His quick affirmation left her speechless. She stared at him, mentally calculating what time she would arrive back in Knoxville if she left right away. Then she saw the corner of his mouth twitch as he tried to hide his amusement. When he laughed outright, the sound prodded boldly at her temper.

"I fail to see what's so funny," she said coldly.

"Obviously. You do have a sense of humor, don't you, Miss Harper?"

She knew he was deliberately baiting her. But knowing didn't quell the overwhelming urge she felt to vent her anger and give him a solid piece of her mind.

He must have seen what was coming because he took a step back and lifted his hands in mock surrender. "Okay, I apologize. Just don't nail me with those daggers shooting out of your eyes."

She continued to glare at him, trying to decide whether or not to let him off the hook. Amazingly, she was having a hard time not responding to his teasing grin. He had an appealing face, she thought absently, surprising herself even more. His features were strong and lean, but not classically handsome. There were too many rough edges for that. His hair was the truest black she'd ever seen. It fell thick and unruly across his forehead now that the baseball cap was gone, and brushed the back of his neck close to the collar of his sweatshirt. But it was his eyes that had immediately captured her attention and continued to intrigue her. No man deserved eyes that blue or lashes that dark and long. His were eyes a woman might be tempted to drown in.

That thought caused her to mentally stumble. Where had that bit of romantic nonsense come from? Disgusted with herself and feeling strangely agitated, she turned and started toward the store entrance. "Come on. Let's get this over with."

She sensed, rather than saw him fall into step beside her. They were nearly to the automatic doors when someone called his name. He looked over his shoulder, then stopped. Ashley paused also and watched as a young woman with a toddler at her side made their way toward them.

Ashley judged the child to be no more than three. She wore miniature jeans and a t-shirt with Mickey Mouse on the front. Tiny red sneakers peeked out from the bottom of her pants, and yellow ribbons secured shiny auburn curls into pigtails.

"Hi," Justin greeted warmly as he took a few steps toward the pair. A delighted grin lit the child's face as she pulled free of the woman's hand and lifted pudgy arms to Justin.

"Love of my life!" he declared as he swung the small bundle high into the air. Childish giggles and masculine laughter blended and filled the air.

Ashley found herself unexpectedly touched by the way Justin related so easily to the little girl. So dogs and children seemed to love him. Reluctantly, Ashley wondered if she needed to revise her opinion of him.

"Hi." The woman came to stand beside Ashley and extended her hand. Her hair, a shade brighter than the little girl's was caught back in a long French braid. She was petite, the curves beneath her snug jeans and blue plaid shirt generous. "I'm Jessi Miles."

"Ashley Harper."

"Sorry," Justin apologized, turning to them. "I forget all my manners when I'm in the presence of such blinding beauty." He smiled into the little face even with his own. "This little lady is Angela Miles. And I'm going to marry her when she grows up."

Angela nodded her head enthusiastically, the idea apparently one she heartily approved of. "I'm going to marry Justin," she stated before planting a sloppy kiss on his cheek.

"See?" He grinned. "It's already decided."

"I don't think you've sold her father on that idea just yet," Jessi warned dryly.

"Ah, we're not worried about him, are we, Angie?"

She shook her head, setting red curls bouncing against her shoulders. "Daddy likes Justin."

"Sure he does." Justin turned his attention to Jessi. "Where is the old man anyway?"

"Planting up on Hunter's Ridge. Corn this year."

"He's had good weather for it."

"So far so good." She smiled at Ashley and then reached for Angie. "We better get going. We didn't mean to keep you."

"It's okay," Justin assured her, releasing the child into her arms. "We're just picking up some things for Ashley. She'll be staying at the cabin for the next ten days."

"You must be an avid angler," Jessi remarked, settling Angie comfortably onto her hip.

"Actually, I've never picked up a pole in my life," Ashley admitted.

Jessi's green eyes flashed with surprise. "You've never been fishing, and you're going to spend ten days here?"

Ashley laughed softly. "I guess you'd call it a crash course. I want to learn to fish, and I want to learn fast. I figured this was the best way."

"Why are you doing this?" Justin asked. "Your dad didn't say."

She shrugged lightly. "Let's just say I have my reasons."

"Well, you've come to the right place," Jessi assured her. "Justin is the best."

"And I don't even pay her to say nice things about me."

"Well, in this particular case I can say it honestly," Jessi teased.

"You wound me." His attention drifted back to Angie. He tweaked her chubby cheek, causing her to giggle and hide her face against her mother's neck.

"Let's get a move on, kiddo. Daddy will be looking for his supper before long." Jessi shifted her bundle to the other hip and looked up at Justin. "Will we see you Sunday afternoon as usual?"

"Sure. Ashley, too."

"Of course. You know it's a standing invitation." She turned to Ashley. "Please come."

"I don't want to intrude—"

"Are you kidding?" Justin scoffed. "This woman cooks for a small army on Sundays. What's one more mouth to feed?"

Ashley sent him a level look before turning to Jessi. "Thank you. Can I bring anything?"

"Oh, no. Don't worry about it." She smiled warmly. "We'll see you then."

Goodbyes were exchanged, and Jessi started off toward the parking lot. Angie peeked over her mother's shoulder, her little hand opening and closing in a farewell wave.

Ashley looked at Justin and found him grinning as he returned the gesture. "I may have to revise my opinion of you," she said thoughtfully.

He dropped his hand back to his side and slid her a glance filled with amusement. "Oh, you don't want to rush into anything."

They gazed at one another a long moment, something odd and unfamiliar vibrating just below the surface. Despite it, Ashley found herself smiling. "Yeah, you're right." Turning, she walked into the store, leaving him to follow.

Chapter Two

Ashley woke early Saturday morning to a thunderous chorus of nature's music. She suspected every bird in Tennessee had taken up residence in the surrounding trees just to serenade her.

After slipping out of bed, she went directly to the kitchen to set a kettle of water to heat on the ancient stove. Justin had said they'd get an early start this morning. She had no idea what he considered early, but she intended to be ready and waiting when he arrived. Stifling a yawn, she headed for the shower.

Fifteen minutes later she emerged dressed in a faded green sweatshirt, worn jeans, and bare feet. With her damp hair caught up in a thick towel, she hummed a tune as she poured steaming water into a cup and added instant coffee. She took a sip and decided that even though it wasn't as hot as she would have liked, it was warm enough to drink. Carrying the cup with her, she turned and started back to the bedroom.

She was just crossing the living room when a stealthy movement out of the corner of her eye caught her attention. Turning her head, she stopped abruptly, causing coffee to slosh over the rim of the cup.

"Damn!" she swore softly. Carefully, she shifted the cup to the other hand and wiped her damp fingers down her denim-clad leg. Her eyes didn't stray, however, from the eight-legged creature making its way steadily across the living room floor. She stood rooted to the spot, suddenly incapable of taking any kind of action.

An involuntary shiver ran down her spine. A grown woman should be capable of taking care of a pesky little spider. But she couldn't help it. It was a phobia. A fairly severe one. And this spider wasn't a little one. It was a healthy-looking fellow, black and fuzzy.

As she stood there wishing for a broom, or at the very least a thick-soled shoe, her uninvited houseguest continued on an uninterrupted course leading to the bedroom. She'd never be able to sleep in that room tonight if it went in there and disappeared.

A sharp rap on the door caused her to jump and the coffee cup to slip from her fingers as she whirled around. The mug shattered with a crash, lukewarm liquid splattering everywhere, including all over her jeans and feet.

"Ashley? Are you okay?" Justin's concerned voice came through the closed door.

Muttering, Ashley stepped carefully around the broken ceramic pieces and jerked the door open. "You scared the hell out of me!"

Justin lifted his hands in a show of innocence. "What's wrong with you? All I did was knock. Are you always so jumpy?"

"No." She waved her hand absently and turned away. "Come in. I need your help."

Justin hesitated. He wasn't at all sure it was safe to be in the same room with her. Deciding to be brave, he pulled the screen door open and stepped inside. She hovered in the middle of the living room, apparently unconcerned by the mess she'd made, but definitely distracted by something in the bedroom.

He frowned as he studied her. Something had her spooked, that much was obvious. She stared into the other room as if she expected the hounds of hell to come bounding out at any moment.

"Okay." She took a deep breath and turned to him. Immediately, her eyes narrowed. "Don't laugh at me."

He shook his head, completely bewildered. "About what? I don't have any idea what's going on."

"What's going on is in there." She pointed toward the bedroom. "It's about this big around." Her right hand came up and she made a circle out of her thumb and forefinger, not quite bringing them together. "And I hate spiders."

"Spiders?"

"Yes! Don't you understand English? This one isn't just a spider. It's a *big* spider. *Huge.*" She demonstrated again with her fingers.

He nearly laughed and caught himself in time. According to her visual description the spider was growing even as they talked. "A big spider," he murmured as he stepped over the mess on the floor and started toward the bedroom. "Where did you last see this monster?"

"You're laughing at me!"

He turned, putting on his best innocent expression. "No, I'm not. I just know from experience that we get some pretty big spiders out here."

If possible, her dark eyes widened even more. He realized they were the only splash of color in her face. Her skin was just as pale as the white towel wound around her head. It occurred to him then that she was really afraid. More so than the average person.

"Okay," he soothed. "Just tell me where you last saw the spider and I'll get rid of it for you."

"It went under the bed."

Perfect, Justin thought. Probably under the bed and through a crack in the floorboards. But she'd be convinced that it had crawled into her bed and would be waiting for her tonight.

"I'll take care of it," he assured her.

It turned out to be his lucky day. The nasty offender had traveled under the bed and had just emerged on the other side when Justin came around the end of the bed. To Ashley's credit, it was a pretty big spider.

"I found it," he called, crouching down.

"I don't want to see it." From the sound of her voice he could tell that she hadn't come any closer to the room or the fearsome intruder.

"Okay, bud, it's just you and me," Justin whispered as he reached into his pocket and pulled out his handkerchief. In one quick move, he caught the spider in the cloth. Reaching for one of Ashley's tennis shoes, he lifted it and brought it down on the wood floor with a heavy and deadly sounding thud.

He straightened and went back into the living room. "I'll just take this outside."

"You can flush it. I always do at home."

"No, that's okay. I'll dispose of it out here." He pushed the door open and walked down the porch steps. Dudley rose and followed curiously as Justin crossed the drive and went to the edge of the woods. He looked over his shoulder to be certain he was out of sight of the cabin, and then opened the handkerchief. Gently, he nudged the spider onto a tree limb. "You'd better run for your life."

When he stepped back into the kitchen, Ashley was busy cleaning up the spilled coffee. He noticed that she'd wasted no time putting on socks and shoes. He sincerely doubted that he'd see her bare feet again during her stay. She'd also removed the towel and had hastily combed her damp hair.

"All taken care of," he reported.

"Good." She didn't look up from her task. "Thanks."

"You're welcome." He paused a moment. "You do realize that you're a lot bigger than the average spider."

Her hands stilled, and slowly she lifted her gaze to his. "No. I hadn't realize that." Ice coated her words. "Thank you for pointing it out to me."

She went back to picking up the broken cup, and he set free the smile he'd been holding back. It appeared his guest had a highly sensitive weak spot. One she found extremely embarrassing.

He went to the stove and found the water now bubbling. Taking down two mugs, he asked, "How many scoops of instant do you take?"

"Just one."

He made two cups of coffee and carried them both to the table. Pulling out a chair, he sat down to enjoy his coffee and watch as she finished wiping up the floor. She tossed the soiled paper towels into the trash and then washed her hands before joining him at the table.

She reached for a two-pound bag of peanut M&Ms sitting in the middle of the table. After her second handful, he had to ask, "Is that your breakfast?"

She paused and looked down at the colorful candies. "Sure." She pushed the bag toward him. "Have some."

"No thanks."

She shrugged and pulled the bag back. "Suit yourself."

A sensitive silence stretched between them while she worked at depleting the bag of candy. Fascinated, Justin watched. Finally, he said, "Tell me something. Is it only spiders you're afraid of or is it insects in general?"

She pinned him with fuming dark eyes. He was certain it was a look she'd perfected to reduce the average person to a quivering mass of nerves. But he didn't consider himself average, and the challenge she presented was far too entertaining to pass up.

"I'm not overly fond of rodents either," she admitted grudgingly. "What difference does it make?"

"You won't see any mice or rats around here. There's a big tomcat that hangs around and takes care of them. What I was wondering about is how you feel about fishing with live bait."

"Live bait?"

"Yeah. Worms or crickets work pretty well."

She didn't respond, just turned to stare down into her coffee cup.

"Of course we can always use artificial bait if you'd prefer," he offered.

"I'd appreciate that," she returned stiffly, still not lifting her gaze.

"Okay." He considered her bent head as he took another drink of coffee and wondered why she didn't pack up all her baggage and head back to the city where she belonged. What could possibly be so important to her to keep her here? "Can I ask you a personal question?"

She lifted her head and eyed him warily. "You can ask. I reserve the right not to answer."

"Fair enough. I was just wondering why you're doing this. It seems a little out of character to me."

"How would you know? You don't know anything about me."

"No, but you're a city girl—"

"And just because I grew up in the city means I can't learn to fish?"

"No." He stopped and frowned. "Has anyone ever told you that you're very defensive? I didn't say you couldn't learn, and I don't mean to insult you when I say you're a city girl. It's a fact. You are. You don't seem real comfortable with nature."

"Why? Because I don't like spiders or mice or live bait? Spiders and mice are both very common in the city."

"But there's a lot more out here. As a matter of fact, if all the spiders joined together to avenge the treatment of their friend here this morning, we'd both be in trouble."

She shuddered and stood. "I don't want to think about it." She carried her cup to the sink.

"I don't think I know anyone as afraid of spiders as you are."

Her cup came down against the counter with a heavy thump. "Okay!" she snapped, whirling to face him. "It's technically called arachnophobia or better known as the fear of spiders. Hollywood made a whole movie about it a few years ago, which I've never been able to watch. I'm terrified of spiders. It's irrational and I know it, but I can't do anything about it. It's a weakness I can't seem to control. Now that you've had your fun, can we just forget it?"

He gazed at her thoughtfully. "You have no patience for weakness, do you, Ashley?"

"None. Especially my own. I've tried everything to get over this, and I just can't. It's the only thing I've never been able to get any control over. It infuriates me."

"I can see that." He rose and carried his cup to the sink. She didn't move away from the counter as he'd expected. Looking over, he could see that the color had returned to her cheeks, probably more from anger than anything else.

"Everyone has weaknesses," he offered logically. "I break into a sweat every time I have to fly."

She smiled slightly and slid him a look. "Do you fly often?"

"Not if I can drive." He returned her smile. "You never did answer my original question."

"Why I'm doing this?" She hesitated and gazed down at the floor. "My fiancé likes to fish. I thought I'd learn so we'd have something we can do together."

"Why didn't you just ask him to teach you?"

"Geoffrey doesn't have a lot of patience when it comes to explaining things." She shrugged. "I wanted to surprise him."

Justin glanced at her ring-free left hand. "When's the wedding?"

"We haven't set a date yet. We've both been busy with our jobs and things. Maybe late in the summer or early fall."

"Your sense of romance is overwhelming," he returned dryly.

"I don't believe in romance."

As soon as the admission tumbled out, he could tell she wished she could take it back. She cast him a quick look before turning her attention elsewhere. He couldn't help but wonder if she truly believed what she said, or if she needed someone to prove her wrong.

"You don't believe in romance," he said smoothly. "Why?"

"Because I'm twenty-seven years old and I've never seen any proof of it. It's a myth kept alive by love songs and romance novels."

Justin heard the solid certainty in her voice. But he detected a faint defiance in her eyes when she looked at him, as if she fully expected him to dispute her words. He decided not to disappoint her.

"Come on. You're a beautiful woman. Surely you've had a man or two try to sweep you off your feet."

"Oh, sure. But it wasn't romance they were interested in."

He laughed softly. "So instead of waiting for the great love of your life, you're going to settle for a merger."

"Well, what's wrong with that?" She took a few steps away before turning to face him. "Geoffrey and I are right for each other. We enjoy the same things, and we think alike. We should have a solid marriage."

Solid and boring, Justin thought. It shouldn't matter to him what she did with her life. It shouldn't matter that she seemed willing to settle for less than what she could have. But for some unexplainable reason, it did. The fact that it mattered unsettled him greatly.

A little voice in the back of his mind suggested that he had ventured into dangerous territory. He and Ashley would both be better off in the long run if they kept things on a strictly business level. After all, it was her life, and if she wanted to throw it away, that was her business. He was perfectly content with the condition of his own life. He'd be an idiot to get involved in any way with Ashley Harper.

He decided to listen to the voice of reason. "You know, we better get started," he stated, moving toward the door. "I've got everything loaded in the truck. Come over when you're ready."

"Give me ten minutes."

He nodded before disappearing out the door.

Ashley stared at the empty doorway a full fifteen seconds before turning away. What was the matter with her? She was trembling. In fact, her whole world seemed to be shaking. She gripped the back of one of the chairs and closed her eyes.

Maybe it was just a delayed reaction to the spider. But even as she grasped at the handy excuse she knew she was lying to herself. The spider had nothing to do with what she felt now. This feeling could be traced to only one source—Justin Holmes.

She opened her eyes and drew in a deep breath. This was ridiculous. She never reacted to men this way. Never. And there was definitely no reason she should be reacting in any way to this particular man. He was a fishing guide, for heaven's sake. They had absolutely nothing in common.

But that didn't stop her from noticing, and admiring, the way he filled out a worn pair of jeans and faded sweatshirt. It didn't stop her from wanting to watch the light play in his blue eyes as he spoke. It didn't stop her from wondering if his hair was as silky as it looked or his lips as firm.

She groaned softly and mentally smacked herself. "It's called physical attraction," she muttered crossly. "Nothing more, nothing less."

He said she was beautiful. The echo of his words caused her pulse to flutter, just as it had when he'd said the words. The unexpected response further annoyed her. She'd never been affected by idle words of flattery before. She couldn't afford to be affected now. Justin was teasing her. That's all it amounted to. She'd be wise to remember that.

After taking another deep breath and feeling more in control of her emotions and the situation, Ashley headed for the bedroom to finish getting ready. She'd told Justin ten minutes. She'd already spent that long trying to get her head together.

Ashley executed a smooth side cast, exactly how Justin had taught her. The lure landed in the water with a plop, causing gentle ripples to fan out. It was a cast guaranteed to attract the attention of any smallmouth bass lurking beneath the glassy water.

From his position on the opposite end of the boat, Justin emitted an appreciative whistle.

She shot him a cocky grin. "Not bad, huh?"

"Pretty impressive."

"Thank you."

"I'm beginning to think you lied to me. Are you sure you've never done this before?"

"Never." She steadily reeled in her line, jigging, making the bait hop and fall along the bottom of the lake. She cast again, a little further to the right this time.

Leaning back in the swivel seat, Ashley adjusted her

baseball cap before letting her gaze drift lazily over the
scenery. All along the shoreline, trees bared by winter's
harsh winds were starting to hint at the lush green leaves
beneath the buds. Blooming dogwoods added hesitant
splashes of white and pink to the natural canvas and a
sweet scent to the air. A variety of bird songs carried across
the lake while water lapped at the sides of the fiberglass
boat in a soothing rhythm.

She found the serenity relaxing and oddly appealing.
Her enjoyment of the peaceful setting came as a surprise.
Relaxing didn't come easily to her. It was her nature to
keep in motion. But on this particular morning she was
content to sit and bask in the sunshine and solitude.

"It's beautiful here," she said quietly.

Justin sailed his lure across the water with an easy flick
of his wrist. "Fishing isn't just about throwing your line in
the water and catching a fish on the other end. There's
something almost mystical about being this close to nature.
It's hard to explain to someone who's never experienced
it."

"How long have you been a guide?"

"Eight years."

"You must really love it. Do you ever get bored being
so far away from everything?"

He shook his head. "I'm not so far away. I can easily
get anywhere I want to go."

She gasped and sat straight up in her chair. "Justin! I
think I've got something."

"Pull!"

She jumped up, wrapped both hands around the pole,
and jerked it back over her shoulder. Frantically, she began
to reel in her line against the opposing force. Then, as
suddenly as it had tightened, the line went limp.

Confused, she turned to Justin. "What happened?"

He brought in his own line and put the pole aside. "You
didn't set the hook. The fish realized all he had was a
piece of plastic instead of the shad he was expecting and
spit out your lure. Go ahead and reel it in." He moved to
stand beside her.

When she drew the bait out of the water, he reached to

capture it with his fingers. The chartreuse lure was still secure on the jighead.

"Are fish stupid or what?" Ashley asked. "Why would they find something that awful shade of green appealing?"

He laughed softly, a low, deep rumble that seemed to travel directly from him to the pit of her stomach. Her carefully collected thoughts of not more than two hours ago went up in smoke.

"You'd be amazed by some of the things I've caught fish on," he said. "Things look different under water. Part of the appeal of this particular lure is the way it moves in the water. Smallmouth like to feed on shad. When you're jigging this lure along the bottom, it looks like shad to the fish. If they're hungry, they go for it. Your job is to set the hook before the fish realizes he's been tricked." He released the lure. "Go ahead and cast again in the same area."

He moved behind her as she followed his directions. "It's important that you react the instant you feel something tug on your line. It's that split second reaction that's going to drive the hook into the fish's mouth. Another thing you need to know is that you don't have to use your whole body to set the hook. All you have to do is snap your wrist and pull back with your arm." He reached around and closed his fingers on her wrist, demonstrating the movement.

Ashley understood his instructions. She didn't understand the sudden charge of electricity she felt when the solid strength of his chest pressed lightly against her back. His breath gently brushed her cheek, and her heart began to pound like she'd just run a marathon.

Vaguely, she wondered what would happen if she simply released the fishing pole and turned in his arms. How would it feel to press her body against the hard lines of his?

The heat she felt flushing her skin had nothing to do with the morning sun. This heat was generated internally. She blinked quickly, struggling to focus on his instructions instead of on her embarrassing fantasies. She had no reasonable explanation for her wayward thoughts. Silently, she sent up a prayer of thanks that the man standing beside her couldn't read minds.

When Justin stepped back, Ashley continued to cast, methodically sending the lure into the mysterious depths and jigging it along the bottom. She forced herself to concentrate on her technique and not on the man standing a few feet away. She told herself she was just excited about catching her first fish. That explained why her pulse pounded like a snare drum. It had nothing at all to do with Justin.

"How long do we have to do this before we catch something?" she asked after a few minutes when she was sure her voice would sound normal.

Justin chuckled and went back to pick up his rod. "If I could answer that, I'd be a rich man. Fishing isn't an exact science. You do your research, and then you make your best guess about where the fish are. Different fish have different habits."

"Why do you prefer fishing for smallmouth?"

"For me they're more of a challenge. Largemouth bass are more popular with anglers, mainly because of their size. But smallmouth are livelier and stronger and not nearly as trusting as their larger counterparts."

Ashley watched as he cast his lure into the water well away from hers. A black cap sporting the flashy logo of a well-known tournament sponsor shaded his eyes from the reflecting glare on the water. On the surface he looked relaxed, but she sensed the underlying readiness as he waited for the slightest pull on his line.

She sat down again on the swivel seat. "When did you start fishing?"

"When I was fourteen."

"Who taught you?"

"A good friend."

The guarded nuance of his voice intrigued her more than the simple words had. "Do you still fish with your friend?"

"No." The answer had a final ring to it, effectively discouraging any further questions. Ashley found her curiosity piqued, but let the subject drop. It was none of her business and obviously a subject he didn't want to pursue.

She reeled in her line and cast it out again. "Dad told me the record smallmouth bass had been caught here at Dale Hollow, but that the record is being contested."

"That's right. It's stirred up a lot of controversy around here."

"I get the impression people take their fishing seriously in this area."

He chuckled. "You could say that. A lot of folks around here think the new record smallmouth will come from this lake."

"Are you including yourself in that group?"

He shot her a quick grin. "You bet."

A slight tug on her line drew her attention. Quickly, she snapped her wrist and pulled back as Justin had shown her. She felt the heavy resistance and knew she had the hook in this time. Coming to her feet, she began to wind the reel.

"I've got him this time," she declared as she worked to subdue the energetic fish.

Justin came to stand beside her just as the fish jumped and broke water.

"Did you see him?" she cried. "He's huge!"

"Keep your line tight." Justin crouched down at the edge of the boat. "Don't let him shake the hook loose."

Inch by inch, Ashley worked to bring her reluctant catch to the side of the boat. A true battle of wills ensued, but after a few intense moments of struggle she could feel the fish weaken.

Justin leaned out over the edge of the boat, balancing there a moment before reaching down to capture the fish by the inside of its gaping mouth. With the resistance gone, Ashley dropped her pole and sat down in the swivel chair with a exhausted sigh of relief. No one had told her that catching fish was hard work.

Justin turned to her as he held up the blue-green fish for her inspection. "He's a keeper. Not too shabby for your first catch."

"But not a new record?"

"Afraid not. This guy probably weighs about three pounds. To break the record you're going to need to bring in one weighing close to twelve pounds."

"You're kidding! A fish that big would have pulled me in."

"Maybe." After putting the fish in the aerated livewell, he straightened and grinned at her. "Looks like you'll get dinner tonight after all."

Ashley gave a satisfied sigh as she took another bite of the flaky fish Justin had prepared. They were sitting at her kitchen table enjoying the fruits of their labor that day.

"How big was my catch again?" she asked.

"Three pounds, six ounces to be exact." His eyes narrowed. "Write it down, Ashley. This is the last time I'm going to repeat it."

She laughed softly. "You're just jealous. The student outdid the teacher, and the student is a woman. A double blow to your fragile ego."

He shook his head. "Why do you put such emphasis on the male–female thing? Are all the men you know male chauvinists?"

"Don't try to play innocent with me. Men hate to lose. It's part of their genetic makeup. And they hate being shown up, especially by a woman."

Justin chewed thoughtfully while considering her words. "I think hating to lose is just human nature. As far as being shown up, I don't think anyone enjoys it if it's done for that reason." He shrugged. "I really don't mind you catching the biggest fish today. Why should I? I think the whole point of this exercise is that you're *supposed* to catch the fish."

"Okay, so maybe you really don't mind. After all, this is your job. But a lot of men would mind."

"What about your fiancé? Would he?"

She heard the subtle challenge behind his words and didn't immediately respond. Unfortunately, she was afraid that Geoffrey would be a little bent out of shape if she caught the biggest fish. It wasn't a fact she was eager to admit, even to herself.

"You know something, Ashley?" Justin stood and carried his plate to the sink. "When you throw your line into the water, the fish on the other end doesn't give a hoot if you're a man or woman, black or white, young or old. All he cares about is eating."

"I suppose you're right."

Justin washed his plate and silverware and left them in the drainer to air dry. After drying his hands, he turned and leaned back against the counter, looking at her. "You can always become a better angler by learning about what it is you're trying to catch. You can learn it, and you can practice it. But the bottom line is, if the fish you're trying to catch isn't interested in what you're offering him, you're not going to catch him. What it all really boils down to is just a matter of luck. Plain and simple."

Ashley stood and picked up her plate. "Then I guess I was pretty lucky today."

"I guess you were." He moved aside to let her get to the sink. "We'll test your luck again on Monday."

"No lessons tomorrow?"

"A man's got to have a day off. Besides, once you finish feasting at Jessi and Cal's, you won't want to do anything but take a nap."

Ashley watched amusement light his eyes and felt a strange, liquid reaction spread through her. It was a heavy, unfamiliar sensation directly related to the man standing a few feet away. She didn't understand it, and she didn't think she wanted it, but it was there just the same.

Turning, she walked back to the table and began to clear away the rest of the dishes. "What time will we leave tomorrow?"

"Around noon. If it's okay with you."

"Sure, it's fine." She waited until he'd crossed the room to the door before glancing over her shoulder. "Thanks for dinner."

"No problem. I'll see you in the morning."

Ashley listened as he stepped onto the porch and called to Dudley. Absently, she reached for a handful of M&Ms and munched on them while pondering the strange sensations plaguing her.

Chapter Three

The Miles's rambling two-story farm house sat perched on a wooded hillside with lush farmland spreading out below it. Red shutters framed tall windows while a porch crowded with wicker furniture and old-fashioned rockers wrapped around three sides of the house.

When Justin said Jessi Miles cooked for a small army on Sundays, he hadn't been exaggerating by much. The place was brimming with people. Ashley had easily lost track of who belonged to Jessi's side of the family, who belonged to her husband's, and who were just friends.

Cal Miles was a big man with a thick Southern drawl, a reserved manner, and a conspicuous love for his wife and daughter. At one point, Ashley had been shocked to discover that she actually felt a twinge of envy for the love they so obviously shared. After being in Jessi and Cal's company for more than an hour, the lyrics of a love song didn't seem so far-fetched after all.

Three long tables, placed end-to-end and covered in a variety of multicolored tablecloths, were positioned beneath the shade of two giant oak trees. Dinner consisted of crispy fried chicken and home-cured ham, garden fresh vegetables, homemade bread and rolls, and a variety of pies and cakes that all looked like they should win blue ribbons at the county fair.

After a brief, but heartfelt prayer of thanks, the feast commenced. Good food, good company, and good humor all under a cloudless blue sky.

Ashley couldn't remember having a better time. Initially, she'd been a little uncomfortable finding herself in a crowd of total strangers, all of whom acted as if they'd known her all her life. But she soon relaxed, realizing there were no strangers here. Everyone was heartily welcome.

Justin was obviously a favorite among this group. He may have been born a Yankee, but he certainly appeared at home on this little farm in Tennessee. Without a doubt, every female present adored him, whether she was three or ninety-three. He charmed each one in equal measure and flirted outrageously. Yet there wasn't a man within earshot who seemed concerned by his behavior.

Ashley watched from across the table as he settled Angie on his lap with familiar ease and continued to talk with Jessi's elderly father about how well the fish were biting. He was dressed much the way he'd been since her arrival. The only difference today was that he'd traded his faded sweatshirt for a royal blue tee shirt with the Starlight Marina logo on it, and his work boots for a pair of high-top tennis shoes. As usual, the jeans he wore were faded and well worn. The baseball cap was gone, and his dark hair looked like it had been pushed back from his face more than once with impatient fingers.

She studied his profile and again found herself wondering about him. At face value he seemed to be a man perfectly content with his life. But Ashley sensed there was more to him than she'd first assumed. She detected secrets behind his carefree manner.

Secrets she had no business worrying about, she reminded herself firmly as she turned her attention back to her food. It was natural for her to be curious about the man. But curiosity had killed the cat, and she suspected such a fate could await her if she learned too much about Justin Holmes.

After eating, people drifted away from the table in a

dozen different directions. Ashley had just finished a piece of blackberry pie when Jessi dropped down onto the bench beside her.

"Are you doing okay? I see Aunt Myra has been plying you with her award-winning blackberry pie."

"It's wonderful. But if I eat one more bite, I'm going to pop." Already she wished her jeans weren't quite so snug.

"Well, you better get up from this table before Aunt Rose discovers you've had some of Aunt Myra's pie. There's a long-standing competition there."

Ashley immediately pushed to her feet and stepped over the bench. "I'm out of here. I won't be able to wear any of my clothes when I go back to work if I keep this up."

Jessi stood and tugged on Ashley's arm. "Come on. All you need is a walk."

"All I need is a nap."

"After the walk." Jessi smiled as they started away from the table.

Ashley cast one guilty look over her shoulder. "Shouldn't we help clean up?"

"Nah. You're a guest. They can manage without us."

"Do you do this every Sunday?"

Jessi nodded and pushed her long hair behind her shoulder. "Sunday is our family day. We've got the biggest place and plenty of room to spread out. Even in the winter the house is big enough for everyone. After church everybody shows up here with whatever they feel like bringing. We throw it all together and call it dinner."

"Well, the food was fantastic. All of Tennessee's good cooks must be in your or Cal's family."

Jessi laughed. "If you asked any of them, they'd all agree with you, and then probably debate which side had the most. We have a lot of proud cooks in this family. What about your family? Is it big?"

"No. Just my dad and sister."

"This must have been a pretty big shock for you then."

"At first. But everyone is so friendly I feel like I'm at home."

"Good." Jessi smiled at her. "I like everyone to feel at home. That's the idea."

"How long has Justin been a part of your get-together?"

Jessi's brows knit together. "I can't remember," she said with a quick laugh. "It seems like Justin has been around forever, but it's probably only been three or four years. I had a hard time getting him to come at first."

"Why? He seems to fit in so well."

"He's different now than when he first came here."

"Do you know where he's from?"

"New York, I think. He's never really said but I've heard him say things that lead me to think that. When he first settled here, he stayed pretty much to himself. We got to know him when we did some remodeling in the house one winter. Somebody mentioned to Cal that Justin had done some handy work for them and was really good. So Cal talked to him and hired him. He's very talented."

They had walked behind the house and away from the noise of the crowd. A white rail fence cut patterns against the rolling hillsides. The barn, stable, and outbuildings stood off to the north, and the yard sloped downward into an open, flat meadow.

Ashley's attention was caught by the activity in the distance. "What's going on down there?"

"They're setting up for a baseball game. The men against the women."

Ashley arched a brow and looked at the other woman. "Another routine activity?"

"No. We don't do this very often. It gets kind of competitive sometimes."

"Sounds like my kind of game. Who's the reigning champ?"

A smug smile curved Jessi's mouth. "The women."

Ashley laughed. "Definitely my kind of game. Where do I sign up?"

"Come with me. I'm the captain and you're in."

Fiercely competitive better described the game being played in the open field. Ashley loved it. The men didn't cut the supposedly weaker sex any slack. They couldn't afford to. The women had been the reigning champs for the last two games. The men were all suffering from seriously bruised egos, whether they were willing to admit it or not.

The rules of play were only slightly altered. The game consisted of six innings instead of the usual nine, and the umpiring duties were split evenly between Uncle Ray and Cousin Nancy, two relatives trusted to be completely impartial at all times. Other than that, all other rules applied.

The game had been close all along. Now in the final inning the score was tied at six, and the women were up to bat last. One run would allow them to keep the cherished title.

Justin was pitching again this inning as he had the last three. Ashley had to admit he was pretty good. She watched from the sidelines as he warmed up with the catcher.

Fourteen-year-old Mary Sue, the next up to bat, stood off to the side and practiced her swing. She hadn't hit the ball yet, and Ashley hoped the girl's luck was about to change. If Mary Sue could get a base hit, then when Ashley was up to bat after her, maybe she could knock the girl in for the winning run.

Mary Sue's first pitch was called outside. The second one was low, but she swung and chalked up her first strike. She got enough of the third pitch to send it bouncing past Justin and into the shortstop's waiting glove. Through she made a valiant effort, she was tagged out at first base.

Jessi squeezed Ashley's arm. "Go out there and sail one into the outfield."

"I did that once. Cal caught it."

"Well, hit it harder this time. And lower."

Ashley shook her head and laughed. "Sure. Whatever you say, coach."

Ashley walked toward home plate and cast a glance in Justin's direction. He stood on the pitcher's mound, his Mets cap in place, and his hands braced on his hips. The cap shaded his eyes, but she knew he watched her every move. Trying to intimidate her, no doubt. Fat chance.

Deliberately, she slowed her pace and put a little more

sway in her denim-clad hips. Looking directly at him, she moistened her lips before honoring him with her most seductive smile. She saw him straighten a little, as if surprised, and knew she'd scored a direct hit. He wasn't the only one who could play dirty.

"Come on, Ashley! Slug that ball!" This bit of encouragement came from Aunt Rose. Ashley supposed she'd have to have a piece of her blackberry pie before she left today.

Taking her stance, Ashley went through one practice swing. As she straightened, an appreciative wolf whistle issued by the pitcher drifted on the air. Ashley didn't immediately acknowledge it, but the spectators did. A few cheers of agreement rose from the men's section, and a few groans of disgust from the women's.

Ashley examined the tip of her bat a moment before turning to look at Justin. He'd pushed the cap back, and she could clearly see the mischief shining in those fantastic eyes. Slowly, she lifted her fingers to her lips and blew him an exaggerated kiss. The crowd erupted into various responses while Justin just shook his head and grinned.

Uncle Ray, who was umpiring, removed his hat and fanned himself a moment. "We'd better get on with this while we can," he teased as he settled the hat back on his bald head. "Batter up!"

The crowd got into it, their voices blending into one continuous blur as Ashley stepped into the batter's box. She took her stance and waited. Justin took his time, dragging out the seconds until his first pitch crossed the plate. Strike one.

Ashley saw his satisfied smile and became only more determined to hit the ball out of the playing area. His second and third pitches were both high and to the outside. She got a piece of the fourth pitch, but it landed foul. The next came across low.

Full count. She stepped out of the batter's box and took a deep breath. The next pitch would be the deciding factor. She tapped the bat against the side of her tennis shoe before turning her attention to Justin. Their gazes met and held. She could see that he was as determined to strike her out as she was to get a decent hit.

She stepped back into the batter's box and took her stance. And waited. Justin hesitated, shifted, and then set himself for the pitch. The instant it left the mound Ashley knew it was hers. The force of the impact stung her hands, and the crack of ball against bat rang out like a firecracker.

She ran on instinct, rounding first and heading for second without any real knowledge of where the ball had landed. As she tagged second and moved on to third, she heard Jessi urging her to keep going. About halfway between third and home plate, she saw Justin sprinting toward the base to cover it. Knowing the ball had to be on the way, she drew on every ounce of energy she had to propel herself forward. She saw him catch the ball and turn toward her in anticipation.

In that split second she decided she just might be able to slide in under him and the ball. Giving no thought to her expensive designer jeans, she waited until the last possible second to hit the dirt. Dust billowed, and she groaned in agony as her foot caught Justin's legs, bringing him down on top of her in a tangle of limbs and dirt and sweat.

She lay for a moment, her eyes closed, gasping for air. The weight on top of her shifted slightly, and she thankfully drew in a deep breath. When her eyes opened, she found herself captured in a deep blue sea outlined by long, dark lashes.

Justin's hat was gone, his face smudged with grime, and his lips only inches from her own. Her heart pumped furiously from exertion and from something primitive and completely foreign to her. In the fog clouding her mind she heard Uncle Ray declare her safe. But she knew better. She felt anything but safe being this close to Justin.

"Are you okay?" He was winded, breathing as hard as she.

"I think so. Are you?"

He shook his head, and she saw a strange flare of light leap into his eyes. "I may never be okay again."

Before she could question his cryptic reply, he rolled

away from her to push to his feet. Slowly she sat up, and he reached a hand down to her. His fingers closed around hers, pulling her to her feet. She winced as she caught her balance and a sharp pain shot through her leg.

"Ashley?"

"I'm okay," she assured him before being engulfed by the rest of the team. The women had won again, and she was the hero of the day.

The sun was setting when Justin pulled the Blazer into the carport and cut the engine. Ashley climbed out carefully, trying to baby her bruised leg without appearing to do so.

"You are hurt," Justin accused as he came around the back of the vehicle. "I didn't have time to brace myself when you took me down. I wasn't hurt because you broke my fall."

"I'm okay," she insisted through clenched teeth.

"Like hell. Where does it hurt?"

He stood directly in front of her, blocking her path. She wanted to move around him and stalk off to her cabin, her pride and dignity both firmly in place. But she knew going around him would take six or seven extra steps. Steps she couldn't afford right now.

"My right knee. It's no big deal."

"Have you checked it out?"

"No. I haven't had a chance. It's probably just a pulled muscle or a bruise. Nothing major, I'm sure. Just let me go to my cabin."

He shook his head, and in one swift movement swung her into his arms. "Come on. You need a hot bath."

Instinctively, her arms closed around his neck. She became acutely aware of his strong arms cradling her close to his solid chest. "Put me down," she demanded once her initial shock had passed. "I can take a hot shower at the cabin. And I can walk on my own."

"No, you can't. And I have a whirlpool tub you can use. Don't argue." He pushed the cabin door open and put her back on her feet.

When he flipped on the lights, she blinked and then stared at her surroundings. This wasn't the rustic cabin she'd expected.

The kitchen and living area ran together forming one long room. From what she could see of just these two rooms, he had every modern convenience imaginable. Everything from a state of the art entertainment system to a dishwasher. A far cry from the bare essentials her cabin provided.

"The whirlpool is back here."

His voice broke her trance, and she looked to where he headed down a short hallway.

"Justin, this is silly. I'm going back to my cabin." She turned toward the door.

"Ashley."

He spoke her name softly and with a power that far exceeded a shout. She knew she should ignore him and keep going. If she had any common sense, she'd get out now.

She turned back to him.

"I feel bad enough about all this," he said quietly. "I shouldn't have forced you to slide like that."

"I made the decision to slide, and I took the risk. All you did was play the game the way it's intended to be played."

"Maybe. But I wanted to win pretty badly. Too badly, I think."

They looked at one another, the width of the room between them. "I don't think my foot ever touched the bag," she admitted wryly.

A ghost of a smile crossed his features. "I didn't think so. I think the dust must have gotten into Ray's eyes."

She hesitated a moment and then took a deep breath. "You've really got a whirlpool back there?"

"With six jets. I guarantee you'll feel better after spending some time in it. You might even thank me tomorrow after all the aches take hold."

A brief mental battle raged. Instinct warned Ashley to keep her distance from this man. But her aching body begged her to make use of his offer of comfort. Ignoring common sense, she accepted the use of the whirlpool.

Steam rose from the bubbling water, clouding the glass enclosure and Ashley's mind. She relaxed back against the smooth black porcelain and let the pulsing water soothe her aches and pains. Time slipped away, and she made no attempt to retrieve it.

A sharp rap on the bathroom door interrupted her utopia.

"I went and got you some clean clothes," Justin called. "Can I bring them in?"

Ashley's gaze flew around the room. She knew he wouldn't be able to see inside the fogged glass surrounding the whirlpool, but still there was something unnerving about letting a man she barely knew into a room where she was clad in nothing more than foamy bubbles.

"Come on in," she answered finally.

"I'll leave your things here on the vanity. I went ahead and showered at your cabin, so take your time in there."

"Thanks. It feels wonderful."

"Good. I'll be close by if you need anything."

She listened intently, waiting for the soft click of the door closing behind him before letting out the breath she'd been holding.

It irritated her that she couldn't decide exactly why Justin unsettled her so. Usually, she could define the exact reason something bothered her or pleased her. Yet with Justin, she found herself completely at a loss for some of the peculiar emotions she felt. Sensing that she wasn't quite in control of her own emotions made her edgy.

Closing her eyes, she took a deep breath and tried to relax again. A sudden, totally unbidden image popped into her mind and wavered there before her, taunting and tantalizing. Justin in the whirlpool beside her, his dark hair turned to a shiny ebony by the mist. She saw the water bead on his skin, felt the heated flesh beneath her fingers as they ran over this slick shoulders. Blue eyes devoured her as he leaned closer, his lips parted in anticipation of capturing hers.

Ashley's eyes flew open, and she sprang to her feet. Grabbing a thick red towel, she scrambled out of the water as if it had turned into scalding lava. It infuriated her even more to discover her hands trembling as she tried to secure the towel around her body.

Lord, what had gotten into her? She had never been one to spend her time on idle fantasies. Even as a teenager, she'd never been given to daydreaming about boys. She'd been too busy doing things to waste her time thinking about such nonsense. Now at the age of twenty-seven, she was entertaining romantic visions of herself and a man she barely knew. What was happening to her? She had to be going crazy. There was no other explanation.

Drying quickly, she reached for the clothes lying on he vanity. When she pulled out the peach-colored panties, she felt a slow heat warm her face. Justin had gone through her things. The thought of him touching her personal belongings did strange things to her stomach. She told herself she was being silly as she slipped into the lacy underwear. It just seemed odd because no other man had ever been through her things. Not even Geoffrey.

The thought of her almost-fiancé sent a shaft of guilt slicing through her. Purposely, she called his features to mind. He was a handsome man with neatly trimmed blond hair and blue eyes. Not the same intense blue of Justin's, but nice just the same. Geoffrey was tall, a good two inches taller than Justin. But his body was soft where Justin's was all taut muscle. Again, Ashley could feel the length of Justin's body against hers after the collision at home plate. The position they'd ended up in had been almost loverlike.

"Dammit!" The oath hissed out between her teeth as she jerked the sweatshirt off the vanity. She had to stop this nonsense. Justin Holmes was nothing more than a mere acquaintance, someone she would never see again after next week. Why she kept conjuring up all these ridiculous fantasies was beyond her.

Deciding it was best to think of nothing at all, she continued to dress, pulling on her jeans and tennis shoes. She picked up the brush Justin had brought with the clothes and ran it through her damp hair.

Giving herself a quick going over in the mirror, she had to admit that she did feel better. At least physically. Mentally, she was a wreck.

Pushing the stupid thought away, she bent to retrieve her dusty clothes before emerging from the bathroom. If she'd been uncomfortable in Justin's bath, she found herself doubly uneasy when she stepped into his bedroom. She knew she should just keep moving, but her curiosity got the better of her, and she paused to look around the masculine room.

A king-sized bed covered with a comforter of bold hunter green and navy stripes was centered between two floor to ceiling windows. A few selective nature prints hung on the walls, and the buffed hardwood floors were bare with the exception of a couple of throw rugs. The only other pieces of furniture in the room were an antique rocker with a quilt thrown over the back and a massive six-drawer oak dresser. A reading lamp sat on a small table beside the bed, along with a stack of books, ranging from Stephen King to Dick Francis.

Apparently, Justin Holmes was a simple man with eclectic reading tastes.

She walked over to the French doors across from the bed and looked out. A narrow deck ran the length of the house giving a view of the steep incline below and the surrounding woods. She supposed in the daytime it would be a pretty sight.

Turning back, she paused a moment. The room was comfortable and unpretentious, like the man who occupied it. She liked it.

And the man? Did she like him too?

Instinctively, she shied away from answering that question. It didn't really matter if she liked him or not. He was being paid to do a job and no doubt, being nice to the customer was part of that job. She needed to keep that in mind at all times. Right now, she needed to get out of his room and quit snooping around like a nosy teenager.

She found Justin in the kitchen. He turned from the refrigerator, a soft drink in his hand.

"Feel better?" he asked.

"Yes, thanks. You probably saved my life."

"Well, it's the least I can do considering I'm the one who caused most of your injuries. Would you like something to drink?"

"No, thanks." She edged closer to the door. "I think I'll just go back to my cabin now."

"I'll walk you." He came toward her and reached for a flashlight sitting on the end of the counter.

"Thanks. I'd appreciate that."

Justin looked at her, a frown marring his features. "You sure you're okay?"

"I'm really ready to call it a day. Can we go?" She saw him stiffen slightly and immediately regretted the sharpness that had filtered into her voice.

He inclined his head and gestured with his hand, indicating that she should go on ahead. "Let's go."

When they stepped out onto the porch, Dudley rose and began to wag his tail in greeting. Ashley bent and gently scratched him behind his ear.

"You want to take a walk with us, Dudley?" she asked softly.

"Come on, Dud," Justin commanded as he started down the steps. The dog immediately fell into step beside his master, leaving Ashley no choice but to follow or be left behind.

Justin flipped on the flashlight, aiming the beam down the gravel drive. They were nearly through the shadowy area when Dudley stopped, lowered his head, and began to growl deep in his throat.

Ashley felt a cold sweat break out along her skin as Justin directed the light toward the spot where Dudley's interest seemed to be focused. The beam caught and reflected back from a set of eyes staring out of the murky darkness. The eerie glow had Ashley gasping and stepping back.

Justin caught her arm. "It's okay. It's just a cat."

"How do you know?" she asked suspiciously as he gently urged her forward.

"Trust me. Come on, Dudley." The cat streaked into the light and disappeared under the cabin.

The dog gave one last threatening growl before hesitantly following his master.

Ashley didn't want to admit it, but the feel of Justin's hand curled protectively around her elbow felt wonderful. She didn't know how to explain it, but she felt safe with him. She had never needed a man to make her feel safe before. She was very good at taking care of herself. But somehow, with Justin by her side, her sense of security seemed to double.

He escorted her to her cabin door and waited while she turned on the lights. She turned to where he stood just inside the room. "Thanks," she said with a brief smile.

"It's all part of the service."

His neutral tone served to remind her that there had been nothing personal intended when he'd taken her arm. He was doing his job, taking care of his client. She felt foolishly disappointed.

"Everything should be okay," he said. "If you'd feel better, I could leave Dudley with you."

"No, that's okay. I'll be fine." She didn't need the man or the dog to take care of her. She'd been taking care of herself without help for years now.

"Okay. I'll see you in the morning then." He turned and pushed the door open. "Good night."

"Good night," she echoed.

She closed the door behind him and flipped the lock. For a reason she couldn't even begin to understand, she felt very alone just then. She sighed and rested her head against the door frame. What in the world was Justin Holmes doing to her?

Chapter Four

Fat raindrops were beginning to fall when Justin pulled the Blazer into his carport. He and Ashley just made it to the shelter of the porch when Mother Nature cut loose, and a sheet of rain engulfed the area.

"That was close," Ashley said as they stepped inside the cabin.

"You're going to have to hang out here until it lets up," he said. "Can I get you a soft drink?"

"Sure. That sounds good."

He walked into the kitchen as she moved restlessly to the screen door to watch the rain. She wished she could give a name to this edginess that had claimed her body and mind. It was as if she were on the brink of something, but she had no idea what. It concerned her that it was somehow linked to her strange reaction to Justin.

For the past two days he'd been nothing more than politely professional. He behaved exactly how she expected him to, yet she still found her mind drifting in directions that both fascinated and frightened her. She'd even considered cutting her stay short. Better that than to embarrass herself.

"Here you go." Justin came up beside her, extending a cold can of soda.

"Thanks." She took it from him and popped the top open.

He leaned an arm against the doorjamb. "Has it let up any?"

"Nope. Looks like our good weather has run out."

"Looks like." He shifted slightly causing his shoulder to brush hers. Ashley felt the light contact shoot through her and stepped back abruptly. Justin turned his head to look at her, frowning. Their gazes met and held.

"Are you okay?" His low-pitched voice vibrated deep inside her. "You've been jumpy all day."

"You're right," she agreed, striving to sound casual. "I think I must be going through work withdrawal or something. I don't normally take this much time off at once."

His brow rose. "It's only Tuesday. You never take two days off?"

"I own my own business, too. As I'm sure you know, it's hard to take time off when you're the owner, the boss, and the hired help."

"What kind of business is it?"

"A gift shop. We specialize in collectibles, but carry other products like greeting cards and such."

He smiled. "I pictured you in an executive type position."

"Up until three years ago I worked for a marketing firm in Knoxville. I'd reached a point where I wasn't thrilled with the job and was ready for a change. I'd always wanted to have my own shop, so my sister and I got together, pooled our resources and knowledge, and came up with Collectibles and More. It's worked out well for both of us."

"So Sara is running things this week while you're here?"

Ashley nodded and then paused. "How do you know my sister's name?"

He hesitated before shrugging. "I met your sister once. A long time ago."

This information came as a complete surprise to Ashley. "When?"

He took a deep breath and pushed away from the door. For a moment, she didn't think he was going to answer

her question. She sensed his reluctance, saw a play of
emotion in his eyes.

"It was the summer after your mother died," he said.
"I spent that summer with your dad. Sara came home from
your grandparents the day I left." He shrugged again and
moved into the kitchen. "I met her then. I'm sure she
doesn't remember."

Ashley watched his retreating back as she mentally
worked to fit the pieces of an obscure puzzle together.
She'd only been six that summer. It wasn't a time she
remembered clearly. But it seemed odd to her that her
father hadn't mentioned Justin spending time with him.

"How did you come to be with my father?" She trailed
Justin to the kitchen, unable to let the subject rest until
she fully understood.

He shot her an impatient look. "I'd run away from
home. I made it as far as Knoxville, at which point my luck
ran out, and I was beaten and robbed. Instead of calling
my father, I called yours. He gave me a place to stay for
the summer."

Ashley shook her head. "I still don't understand. How
did you know to call Daddy?"

"Because I'd met Nick. He and my father were fraternity
brothers in college. They'd stayed friends over the years.
They're still good friends today."

Surprise rocked her. "You're J.T.'s son?"

"Guilty."

"Does your family know where you are?"

"No," he shot back sarcastically. "I believe they've
reported me missing. I'm sure my picture has appeared
on milk cartons across the country."

"I just meant—"

"I know what you meant." He shook his head and gave
a short, humorless laugh. "I'm a big boy, Ashley, and I
tend to do as I please. I'm not hiding out here. People
know where to find me if they want me." He turned away
to look out the kitchen window.

Ashley gazed at his stiff back trying to recall the bits
and pieces of information she knew about Justin and his
background. He was the oldest son of J.T. and Rebecca

Holmes, born in New York City, and heir to the Holmes fortune and multi-million dollar business. Because of some conflict with his father, Justin had walked away from his family and the business several years ago.

She wondered why she hadn't made the connection between Justin and J.T. Shortly after she'd opened Collectibles and More, J.T. had stopped in Knoxville while on a business trip to visit with her father. She'd been pleased and flattered when he'd taken the time to stop by her shop. He'd bought a gift for his wife, his choice carefully thought out. Ashley had liked him instantly.

"Can I ask you a question?" she asked cautiously.

"No." Justin turned and walked out of the kitchen.

His blunt refusal was quick and sure. The slamming of the door after he stepped out onto the porch punctuated his response.

She hesitated a moment before following him outside. She found him leaning against the railing, his forearms resting on the rough wood. The rain fell in a steady, straight curtain, leaving the porch dry.

"Come on, Justin," she chided gently. "What's the big deal?"

"It's old news. Just leave it alone."

His words were laced with bitterness and something else. She thought it might be regret.

"I met your father a few years ago. He bought a gift for your mother. I liked him." She moved to lean a hip against the railing. "It might help if you talked about it, you know."

He continued to stare out into the rain as if her words hadn't been spoken. Then, very slowly, he straightened and turned to face her. The intensity and turbulence of emotion in his eyes startled her.

"I find your sudden interest in me and my feelings fascinating," he said softly. "After all, I'm nothing more than a lowly fishing guide ranking far below your lofty station in life."

"Now wait a minute!" she protested, stung by his words.

"You've been fighting the attraction between us from the beginning because being attracted to a fishing guide doesn't meet your rigid specifications. But all that's changed now, hasn't it, Ashley? I'm not just a fishing guide. I'm the son of one of the richest men in America. Now I'm someone worth knowing."

Ashley had never been so insulted. "Your ego is way out of control, Justin. You better get a grip on it before you embarrass yourself." She barely managed to push the words past the outrage she felt. Abruptly she turned away, fully intending to leave despite the downpour.

"You can't even deny it." His softly spoken accusation stopped her before she took the second step.

She turned back to him. "Deny what? Your delusional, conceited theories don't deserve to be acknowledged one way or the other."

Their gazes locked and held for a heartbeat. Then before she knew what hit her, his fingers snaked out and captured her wrists to haul her body against his own. The force of the impact had the air rushing from her lungs. She looked up into his eyes and was nearly scalded by the brilliant blue fire there. Her hands were trapped against the steel of his body, his face only inches from her own.

"Deny it, Ashley," he commanded. "Tell me you don't feel the heat between us. Tell me you don't want it."

Her mouth opened, but the words never came. She stared into his eyes unable to deny what she wanted more than life right now. Emotion rushed at her from every direction, battering her fragile control, tearing at her very soul. She still didn't understand. She just knew she hovered on the brink of discovering something more powerful, more wonderful, than life itself. And it seemed that the only person who could reveal the mystery for her was this man.

"I can't," she whispered. Did he have any idea what that admission cost her? She hated being weak. But God help her, standing against him now, she was as helpless as a newborn baby.

She saw the change in his eyes, saw the banking of the fury and felt the gentling of the fingers biting into her flesh. And then he bent toward her. With his lips just a breath from her own, she heard him murmur, "I can't deny it either."

His mouth claimed hers without any hesitation, and she responded with a hunger she would have considered embarrassing if she'd been thinking clearly. But clear thinking had no place here. Feeling was the only thing necessary. And she was feeling things now that she'd never imagined before.

A delicious, all-consuming heat coursed through her body. When his hands came up to frame her face, his touch seared her skin. Her hands slipped around him, pushed under the soft cotton of his sweatshirt to press into his back. His warm flesh and smooth muscle flexed beneath her searching fingers.

He deepened the kiss, and she opened to him, wanting him to take all she had to offer. His hands roamed over her shoulders and down her back until they came to rest on her hips. He shifted slightly, urging her hips into intimate contact with his. Instinctively, she arched her body to his. She heard his groan and felt a surge of primitive power. The world was spinning out of control, and she didn't care. All she wanted was more. She wanted it all.

After several delightfully blurred moments, he finally lifted his head. She leaned into him, burying her face against his neck as her hands moved restlessly up and down his back.

This is wrong. The wispy thought drifted through Ashley's hazy brain. In defense, she pressed closer to him, rubbing her cheek against his sweatshirt, drawing in the scent of him. How could something that felt so right be wrong? she argued with herself. Then an image of Geoffrey came into clear focus, and she knew.

Coming abruptly to her senses, she pushed away from Justin. He released her without resistance. She stepped back, first one step, then another, until there was a healthy distance between them. Still she felt her skin heat under his sharp gaze.

His hair was mussed, his shirt bunched around his waist. Had she done that?

Feeling the tickling brush of hair against her cheek, she reached up to push it behind her ear. She was amazed to find her hair hanging freely to her shoulders, the elastic band that had been holding it back now gone.

"Here it is." Justin extended his hand, the red band resting on his palm.

She stared at it. He'd taken it, freed her hair, and she hadn't even known? The knowledge shook her. Instead of reaching for it, she backed away another step.

"I have to go." Her voice sounded faint.

"It's still raining."

"I don't care. I can't stay here with you."

He frowned. "Why? I'm not going to hurt you."

Ashley couldn't even form a reply. He'd just shaken the very foundation of her life. Everything she'd ever believed about herself now seemed in question, and he stood there calmly assuring her that he wasn't going to hurt her. Didn't he know that there was no way for him not to hurt her now?

"Come on, Ashley," he said briskly as he strode toward her. Before she could move, he reached for her hand and dropped the band onto her palm. He reached up and brushed his knuckles against her cheek. "Don't look so stunned. It was only a kiss."

With that he turned and walked into the cabin. Slowly, she reached up to touch her cheek. She could still feel his touch there.

Only a kiss? She'd been kissed plenty of times and none of them had ever come close to this. It hadn't been only a kiss. It had been a revelation.

Justin watched from the kitchen window as Ashley hurried along the drive and disappeared into the woods. It was still raining hard and he knew she'd be soaked by the time she got to her cabin. But it was just as well that she'd gone now. He wasn't in any shape to deal with her and what had just transpired on the porch. Although he'd hidden it well, he'd been just as affected as she. And he didn't want it any more than she did.

He closed his eyes and dropped his head. God, what a royal blunder. He'd handled that whole scenario badly.

Why had he allowed himself to go on the defensive when she'd discovered his identity?

Sighing, he lifted his head to stare again at the steady rainfall. He'd spent his whole life witnessing the way people automatically changed before his eyes when they discovered he was J.T.'s son, the heir apparent. From an early age it had infuriated him, but he'd learned to deal with the frustration, understanding there was nothing he could do to change who he was or how people chose to perceive him. He could never shake the feeling, however, that he had no identity of his own. He'd often wondered how many of his successes were truly his own and not a reflection of his father.

The problem with his encounter with Ashley was that he'd forgotten how to deal with the frustration. Since coming to Windsong he hadn't encountered one person who knew him to be anything other than a simple fishing guide trying to build a stable business.

Of course, all of that could change now that Ashley knew the truth. As one of the wealthiest men in America, J.T. Holmes had a very public profile. Justin knew how quickly the news that J.T.'s son had been masquerading as a fishing guide in their area would spread through the Windsong community. He could well imagine the curious glances that would be directed his way, and the curious questions from those who were brave enough to ask. People who had little found it difficult to understand how someone who had more than their fair share could be unhappy with their fate. Everybody said money couldn't buy happiness, but few really believed it. Justin did.

"Damn," he muttered, turning away from the window to move to the refrigerator. He pulled a soda out and popped the top, pausing to take a long swallow before walking into the living room and dropping into the wide recliner.

Dudley lifted his head from his position at the side of the chair and gave a tentative wag of his tail. Absently, Justin reached down to give him an affectionate pat.

Justin figured he probably didn't need to worry about Ashley blowing the whistle on him. After all, who was she likely to tell? She'd be gone in less than a week, so what would be the point of her telling anyone?

If he wanted something to worry about, all he needed to do was think about the feelings Ashley stirred in him. His time would be better spent worrying about how to get through the rest of the week without becoming any more involved with her than he already was.

The reason he didn't need to get involved with her numbered many. The first of which was the fact that she was already engaged. Or at least that's what she claimed.

A smug smile curved his mouth. He couldn't help but wonder if her fiancé knew about the fire simmering just beneath her cool exterior. Judging by her reaction a few minutes earlier, Justin doubted that the other guy had a clue. Ashley had been stunned by her uninhibited response. Stunned and then embarrassed. There was no way her fiancé had elicited that response from her before.

Hell, her response had stunned him. Justin had felt the attraction between them from the beginning, but never in his wildest dreams had he thought the combustion could be so spontaneous or so hot. He could still feel the slender length of her body molded almost perfectly to his own, all that sizzling heat just below the surface. He could have swept her into his arms and carried her into his bedroom, could be making love to her right now with the rain dancing upon the roof.

Swearing soundly, he stood and looked around for the keys to the Blazer. He'd be damned if he was going to sit here and work himself into a lather over a woman who was going to disappear from his life in five days and never return. Physical attraction was a trap he could do without.

He located his keys and left the house. It looked like the rain had settled in for the day. Perfect weather for a beer and a few rounds of pool at the Southern Comfort pub in town.

It was just physical, Ashley told herself for the umpteenth time. So Justin had a way with women. He'd probably been practicing for years. Well, she wasn't going to become another notch on his bedpost.

A vision of that big bed in his room drifted in front of her eyes. Along with it came rumpled sheets in the moonlight and a fresh breeze through the French doors. And Justin.

She jumped to her feet, grabbed a handful of M&Ms and restlessly began to pace the length of the kitchen as she munched. What in the world was the matter with her? She had never acted like this in her life. At this late stage she was allowing herself to be seduced by fantasies of a man she didn't even know. It was a physical attraction and nothing more. And she was overreacting to the whole thing.

All night long she'd tried to work everything out in her mind. She couldn't have gotten more than a couple of hours of sleep. Now, even though the clock indicated it was well into the morning, a deep gloom hung over the cabin. The rain had let up sometime in the night, but clouds still threatened.

She wished she could think straight, but she was still as muddle-minded as she'd been yesterday afternoon when the earth had moved and life as she knew it became an unexpected puzzle. It was all so frustrating.

Pacing to and fro, she tried to force some logic back into her thought waves. She was engaged to Geoffrey. Well, almost, she amended. Maybe she wasn't officially engaged, but she knew she wanted to marry Geoffrey. No, she was going to marry him, no doubt about it. He was perfect for her. Handsome, hardworking, dependable and . . . safe.

Sure, but does he make your heart melt and your senses sing?

Ashley stopped and blinked. Where had that niggling little romantic voice in the back of her mind come from all of the sudden? She was sure about her feelings for Geoffrey. No, her heart didn't melt and her senses didn't sing when he kissed her. But so what? Better to settle for a lasting, solid relationship than one based solely on physical fireworks. That's all she and Justin had in common. A strong physical attraction bound to fizzle out at some point.

She began to pace again, satisfied that she was finally thinking clearly. Geoffrey was the right man for her. No doubt about it. Nothing had changed really. Nothing that would damage her relationship with her fiancé. She'd shared a kiss with Justin, nothing more. She'd allowed herself to be swept away, but only for a moment. It was all clear in her mind now. She could handle this.

Everything was under control. She was fine.

The knock on the door had her swinging around, nearly toppling a glass off the counter. With her heart pounding, she peeked out the window. An illogical mixture of disappointment and relief washed over her when she saw her visitor wasn't Justin. Walking over, she opened the door for Jessi and Angie.

Jessi smiled as she stepped into the cabin. "Are we interrupting anything?"

"No. Just me going stir-crazy. Isn't this a lousy day?"

"Pretty dreary. Justin said you wouldn't be fishing today. I thought I'd stop by to see how your knee is."

Ashley waved a dismissive hand. "Just a bruise. Nothing to worry about. Come on in and sit down. Would you like a cup of coffee?"

"Sounds great." Jessi sat at the table and settled Angie on her lap. After looking around she gave a short laugh. "This isn't a bad cabin if you haven't seen Justin's."

"Yeah." Ashley carried two steaming cups to the table and sat down. "He certainly has all the creature comforts."

"Well, it's his home. I guess that makes the difference."

"Will we see Justin?" Angie asked hopefully, looking up into her mother's face.

"I don't think so, honey. He said he had some errands to run today."

"I thought you said you talked to him," Ashley said.

"On the phone. I called him to check on you. Since I knew you were going to be cooped up here all day, I thought I'd stop in to see if you wanted to spend the day at our place."

"We're gonna bake cookies!" Angie exclaimed, her eyes shining as she smiled at Ashley.

"Yeah," Jessi agreed. "We're going to bake some cookies, aren't we?"

Angie nodded vigorously, her red curls bouncing. "Can Ashley help?"

Something Ashley had never felt before, another new emotion and one she couldn't give a name to, stirred deep within her. Gazing at the child, she had the sudden urge to hold the small bundle of energy in her own arms. It was almost an ache.

Shifting her attention to Jessi, she smiled. "I'd love to help you bake cookies today."

Angie cheerfully clapped her hands. "Chocolate chip!"

With a laugh, Jessi hugged her daughter. "Chocolate chip are her favorite. I hope you like them."

"I love them," Ashley assured them.

"Are these enough chocolate chips, Angie?" Ashley tilted the large mixing bowl so the little girl could see inside.

"More!"

"You think so?" Ashley picked up the bright yellow bag of semi-sweet morsels and sprinkled a few more into the bowl. Again she stirred the stiff batter with a wooden spoon before shifting the bowl for Angie's inspection.

Angie nodded her approval, her eyes bright with joy. Ashley reached out and touched a soft cheek, stroking the baby-soft skin.

"Is she always so happy?"

"Always," Jessi said as she wiped spilled flour from the countertop. "She just has a happy nature. She loves everyone and everything and rolls with the punches."

"I'd guess she gets that from you."

Jessi smiled. "Pretty much. Cal tends to be moody. When something is bothering him, he clams up and has to work it out by himself. Angie and I just let it all hang out."

"How long have you and Cal been married?"

"It'll be nine years in September."

"You must have been very young."

"I was seventeen. But I knew I wanted to marry him when I was fourteen."

"Fourteen?" Ashley couldn't conceal her disbelief. She thought of her own life at that age and couldn't remember being sure of anything. "How could you be certain at that age?"

Jessi shrugged and dried her hands on a dish towel. "I can't explain it to you. It was just something I knew. Cal was two years ahead of me in school. We started dating when I turned sixteen, but I'd had a crush on him for years. I was sure I wanted to spend my life with him."

Ashley had a hard time understanding the concept of being that certain about wanting something. In her own life she'd wanted a lot of things only to discover that once she had them, they weren't what she'd wanted after all. She'd done a lot of things searching for a sense of satisfaction. She'd truly enjoyed many of those things. But a true satisfaction never came as a result.

"Are you still sure?" she asked.

"Positive."

"But is this all you want for yourself? You're a wife and a mother, and those are wonderful things. But is there anything you want just for yourself? Do you have a dream just for yourself?"

"Sure I do. I love to do ceramics. I've even designed some things myself." She shrugged out of the red-and-white gingham apron and draped it over a chair. "Someday I'd like to have my own shop. Cal set me up a workplace in the basement. I have everything I need and I've started to do some research. I hope to sell some of my designs."

"And Cal backs you on this?"

"Of course. He hasn't fenced me in here, Ashley. This is where I want to be. Cal and Angie are the most important things in the world to me."

"Cookies!" Angie stood between the two women, clutching a metal baking sheet nearly as big as she.

Her mother laughed and bent to scoop her into her arms. After planting a noisy kiss on her tender cheek, she turned to sit her on the counter. "You're right. Ashley and

I have gotten sidetracked when we could be enjoying warm cookies right now."

"What's the next step?" Ashley asked as she carried the bowl of dough to the counter.

"We just take a teaspoon and drop the batter onto the cookie sheet like this." Jessi dug a spoon out of the silverware drawer and demonstrated the technique of creating the perfect cookie. Once she had four even rows, she opened the oven and slid the tray inside. "Now," she said, reaching for Angie, "comes the hard part. We have to wait."

Angie giggled as her mother lifted her high into the air.

Chapter Five

Ashley soon became a true believer that few things in life were better than a chocolate chip cookie warm from the oven. How she'd missed this simple pleasure was a mystery to her. She'd taken cooking classes, but most of the things she'd learned were more along the lines of gourmet food. Nothing came close to the simple delight she'd discovered this rainy afternoon inside a cozy country kitchen.

When all the baking was done and the mess cleared away, Jessi carted a tired Angie off for her afternoon nap. Ashley carried a couple of cookies and a glass of iced tea into the living room and curled up in the corner of a large overstuffed sofa.

She took a sip of her drink and looked around the comfortable room. Sturdy, no-frills furniture gave it a natural, lived-in look. Muted light coming through the tall windows added warmth even on such a dreary day. The sound of rain on the roof was accompanied by the rhythmic ticking of the clock on the fireplace mantel. Ashley found herself thoroughly enjoying the solitude.

Jessi came downstairs a few minutes later to join her. She dropped onto the opposite end of the sofa and kicked off her canvas shoes. "Ah. A couple of hours of peace and quiet."

"Thanks for having me over today," Ashley said. "I've really enjoyed this. And these." She held up a cookie and grinned.

Jessi laughed. "I'll write out the recipe before you leave."

"Is it a family secret like Aunt Rose's blackberry pie?"

"No, it came right off the chocolate chip package with only a minor variation of mine, which I will share with you."

"Good. I want mine to taste just like these."

"They will."

Ashley shifted so that she could rest her head against the backrest. "I can't believe I'm sitting here with nothing to do and enjoying it."

Jessi studied her a moment. "Can I ask you a question, Ashley?"

"Sure."

"Do you know what you're searching for?"

Ashley gave the question serious consideration before answering. "Not exactly. I just know something is missing. I keep trying to find out what it is, but I can't. Nothing I do seems to fill the void."

"Maybe you're doing too much. Maybe you need to stop and let whatever it is catch up with you."

"I'm not good at stopping. It seems sometimes that I'm always doing something."

"But you're doing nothing now and enjoying it," Jessi pointed out. "It's easier to slow down when you're out somewhere like this. We don't have the pressures of the busy city here. Maybe you need to get away more often."

"I have enjoyed my stay here. I thought it was going to be hard at first, but I've found that I really enjoy the solitude. There's been a lot of things about this trip that have surprised me."

Ashley was tempted to tell Jessi about all the confusion she felt associated with Justin, but held back. The emotions were so new and unfocused she wasn't sure she could even adequately explain them. Besides, she'd be gone in a few days. Once she got home, she figured she'd finally be able to settle all her ambiguous feelings about Justin.

"After you go back to Knoxville, if you feel like you want to come back for a few days, you're welcome to stay here," Jessi said. "We have an extra bedroom that's available anytime you want to use it."

Ashley was touched by the sincere offer. "Thank you. I just might do that."

"I hope you do." Jessi smiled and reached over to pull the homemade afghan off the back of the sofa. "Here. Why don't you snuggle up with this and take a nap. You look like you could drop off at any moment. Might as well be comfortable."

"I'm not a very good guest," Ashley said ruefully as she reached for the blanket. "I didn't sleep well last night and this is perfect nap weather."

Jessi nodded as she stood. "Nothing like a gentle rain to soothe the soul. Enjoy your nap. I'm going to go downstairs and work some."

"Thanks," Ashley murmured as she settled deeper into the sofa and the welcoming arms of sleep.

Justin had thought it all out carefully the evening before. He'd decided the only way to handle Ashley was to pretend nothing out of the ordinary had happened. That had seemed like keen logic at two in the morning with his head a little fuzzy from lack of sleep. Now, as he pulled into the Miles's driveway, he hoped his reasoning still held when he saw Ashley.

He parked the Blazer behind Jessi's car and made a dash through the pouring rain to the shelter of the back porch. He knocked once before opening the door to let himself into the quiet house. Recognizing the lingering scent of chocolate chip cookies, he went directly to the cookie jar to help himself. He then crossed the kitchen and stepped into the living room.

And that was where his carefully crafted logic of the night before took a flying leap out the window.

On the sofa, Ashley slept, her cheek pressed into a pillow

and one arm curved protectively around Angie who was snuggled up against her. The reaction Justin felt deep inside was painfully intense. In less time than it took for lightning to strike, he recognized what was missing from his life. In an instant everything fell into place. It was no longer a matter of what he did or didn't want. It was a matter of what he needed. This woman, a child, a home.

As he stood there, Angie's eyes opened and a sleepy smile appeared. He moved closer to the sofa and placed a finger to his lips. "Don't wake up Ashley," he whispered.

"Cookie?" Angie pointed to the one he still held.

"Yeah. Come on. I'll share with you."

Angie squirmed out from under the restraining arm.

"Hey," Ashley protested sleepily. "You were keeping me warm."

"Here." Angie turned and spread her soft baby blanket over Ashley's shoulders. "My blankey will keep you warm."

Ashley smiled, taking a moment to bask in the peaceful feeling washing over her. She opened her eyes and reached up to brush her fingertips against the child's silky hair. "Thank you, Angie."

"Justin has cookies!"

It wasn't until Angie turned to point that Ashley realized they weren't alone in the room. She hadn't heard Justin come in, but there he stood, a few feet away, staring down at her. She couldn't describe the look in his eyes even though she felt the full impact of his gaze at the very center of her soul.

He moved closer and knelt at the edge of the sofa. Ashley could hear her heart beating out a quick rhythm of confusion and anticipation as he gently brushed the hair back from her forehead and cheek. With one fingertip he tenderly traced the curve of her lips. Her eyes closed briefly as her composure threatened to slip away. She knew she needed to do something, anything to break the spell he'd cast. But when she opened her eyes, he was bending toward her, and logic and common sense were only words without meaning.

With the exception of his hand resting against her cheek, he didn't touch her otherwise. The kiss was tender, almost chaste, and the unexpected beauty of it brought tears to her eyes. Never in her life had she felt so cherished and protected. It wasn't something she could explain. It was something she felt deeply and with great certainty.

He lifted his head and she stared into his eyes searching for something to explain why he could make her feel so vulnerable.

The sound of childish laughter edged its way into her mind, and she sat up slowly as Justin stood and scooped Angie into his arms.

"What are you laughing about?" he demanded playfully.

"You kissed Ashley!"

"I did?" He opened his eyes wide in mock surprise. "Are you sure?"

Angie nodded vigorously. "I saw you!"

"What's all this?" Jessi entered the room. "Justin, did you come in and wake everybody up?"

"Looks that way."

"Justin kissed Ashley!" Angie declared.

"Oh, really?"

Ashley looked away from Jessi's curious glance and began to fold the afghan.

"Just a little peck on the cheek," Justin stated.

"No!" Angie shook her head sharply. "Here." She placed her fingers against Justin's lips.

Jessi laughed and reached for her daughter. "Justin, don't you know you can't get away with anything when there's a three-year-old in the room? They repeat everything they hear and recount everything they see. And they remember every detail."

"I'll keep that in mind."

"I want a cookie," Angie stated.

"Let's wash up first," Jessi answered as she started toward the stairs.

Ashley felt the weight of Justin's gaze as she continued to straighten an already neat sofa. She nearly jumped out of her skin when his hand touched her shoulder. Jerking away, she turned to face him. "No more of this," she said, striving to keep the panic she felt from sounding in her voice.

His eyes narrowed as he studied her. "I'm sorry if I embarrassed you—"

"I'm not embarrassed. I just don't like games, Justin, and I won't play this one with you."

"What the hell are you talking about? What game do you think I'm playing."

She drew in a breath that sounded precariously close to a sob. Determined not to cry, it took every ounce of strength she possessed to reel in her emotions. "I don't know what you're doing, but I don't like it. You know I'm engaged."

"Just how engaged are you?" He took a step toward her. "You don't wear his ring. You've been here almost a week and haven't bothered to make one phone call to him. What kind of man lets his fiancé go off alone for ten days to a secluded area like this?"

"He didn't know where I was going."

"Why? Didn't he care enough to find out? Trust me, Ashley, if you were engaged to me, there'd be a ring on your finger, and I'd know where you were and what you were doing."

"Thank God I'm not engaged to you. With that kind of attitude you'd smother me within a week. Geoffrey trusts me and that's the way I like it. I don't need his ring on my finger. I can be just as engaged without it."

"Can you? Why don't you just admit what's really bothering you?" He took another step toward her, bringing them nearly toe-to-toe.

Ashley didn't back down, although every instinct she possessed screamed for her to do so. "Why don't you tell me what you perceive that to be?"

"What's really bothering you is that no one, not Geoffrey, not another man alive on this earth, has ever made you feel what you feel when you're in my arms."

"How do you carry that ego around with you, Justin? It must get pretty heavy by the end of the day."

"It's not ego, honey, it's fact. You're up against something you can't control. And because you can't control it, you don't want to recognize it as the truth it is. But on this one issue I know you better than you know yourself."

She trembled as emotions tumbled around inside her. Nothing made sense anymore. He made her feel things she didn't understand, things that frightened her. When she was with him, she couldn't tell what was real and what was just her imagination. She hated losing control, and she hated him for backing her into a corner she couldn't fight her way out of.

She shoved him away. "You think you're so damned smart, but you don't know me. I can't deny that on a physical level you arouse me. So what? I'm sure I'm not the first woman you've aroused. It's just a physical response and nothing more. I don't want it, Justin, and I don't want you. Do I make myself clear?"

"Perfectly." He reached into his pocket and pulled out his keys. "I'm going home. Are you coming?"

"No. Jessi will bring me later."

"Fine." He turned and headed toward the kitchen.

"I intend to finish my stay," she called to his retreating back. "And I intend to get my money's worth."

He swung around. "Do you have a complaint so far? Do you feel that you haven't gotten your money's worth?"

She hesitated. "No, I've been satisfied."

"Then what makes you think you won't get what you paid for in the next four days? You won't be cheated, Ashley."

"Thank you," she returned stiffly.

He inclined his head slightly. "Oh, it's my pleasure."

With that he turned and left her standing alone in the middle of the room.

Justin felt a stab of perverse satisfaction when Ashley appeared the following morning looking as tense and edgy as he felt. He hoped her night had been as sleepless as his own.

The short drive to the marina was accomplished in silence. He was easing the boat away from the dock when Ashley finally spoke.

"Where are we going to fish today?"

"A little area called Hickory Cove. I haven't fished it

lately, but I usually have pretty good luck there, especially after a good rain."

Justin noticed that once they'd arrived at the secluded spot and the sun began to warm the air, Ashley began to relax. He would have wished the same for himself.

By mid-morning they'd had a good two hours in the cove, catching and releasing several fish. Justin had taken some time to teach Ashley the proper technique for releasing a fish since neither of them were in the mood to share a fish dinner.

"I like this idea," Ashley said from her place on the opposite end of the boat. "It seems more sportsmanlike to release the fish."

"There's no need to keep them if they're going to be wasted. Besides, if every fisherman kept his quota every time he came out, we'd soon exhaust our supply of fish."

He felt a tap on the end of his line and immediately set the hook. The feisty fish put up a commendable fight before Justin managed to real it in. He knelt and leaned over the side of the boat, capturing the fish by its lip. Carefully, he worked to remove the hook.

"How big is he?" Ashley leaned forward to see.

Justin freed the hook and held the fish up for her. "Three pounds or better I'd guess."

He lowered the fish head first into the lake and gently led it so the water could flow through its gills. He felt it pull away and released his hold. As if to have the last word, the smallmouth gave a sharp slap of its tail, sending a spattering of water in Justin's direction.

He sat back and bent to wipe his face on his shirt sleeve. "I guess he told you."

Justin looked up and found himself dazzled by the smile Ashley directed his way. "Yeah, I guess he did."

Reaching for his rod, he concentrated a moment on adjusting the lure. It didn't really need it, but he needed something to keep his attention focused away from Ashley. He thought he was doing a commendable job of playing the professional fishing guide for her, but the emotional knots she'd tied him in were beginning to take their toll. He'd spent a long night trying to figure out what to do about her. Common sense told him to let her leave his life as easily as she'd come into it. His heart told him to fight for what he wanted. Or needed.

It infuriated him that she could so easily reduce what was between them to a physical level. He remembered trying to do the same thing when they'd first met. It hadn't taken him long, however, to realize that what was between him and Ashley was much more than physical. He didn't just want her in his bed. He wanted her in his life. That admission, even when made only to himself, scared him to death.

"Justin!"

Her startled cry had him twisting around to look at her over his shoulder. He saw her jerk back with a quick pull to set the hook, then watched, amazed as her pole arched downward. She gripped the handle with both hands, struggling to hold onto it, and sent him a desperate look.

Dropping his equipment, he scrambled across the boat, scanning the water in search of whatever she'd hooked. One, two heartbeats passed. And then the fish shot straight up out of the lake. Drops of water sparkled like fat diamonds in the sunlight, momentarily framing the huge smallmouth before it disappeared below the surface again.

At the sight of her catch, Ashley's heart had jumped into her throat. She kept a death-grip on the rod, half expecting the monster fish to pull her into the lake.

"Let him run," Justin instructed. "As big as he is he should tire pretty quickly."

"Great," Ashley muttered, her breath coming fast and hard. "When he's tired, will he just climb peacefully into the boat?"

Justin shot her a quick, amused glance. "I doubt it. Where's your sense of adventure?"

"I think I swallowed it a few minutes ago." She pushed the rod toward him. "Here. You bring him in. I don't think I can."

Their eyes met. "Yes, you can," he said.

The fish jumped again, drawing both their attention. It was further out now and not nearly as energetic. Already it was beginning to tire, as Justin had predicted.

"Start to reel him in," he said.

"Come on, Justin. I can't do it. Just take the rod and bring the dumb fish in!"

He shook his head without turning to her. "It's your catch. You need to bring it in. I'll net it for you."

Ashley figured she had two choices. She could either fight the fish, or she could let the rod go. Neither option agreed with her. She wanted Justin to bring the fish in. She'd seen the excitement in his eyes, could almost feel it radiating from him. This could very well be the fish he'd been waiting for. And by some fluke of fortune it had ended up on her line.

"Start to reel," Justin reminded her sharply. "Don't give him a chance to break the line."

She began the give-and-take maneuver of reeling her line in. She'd land the damned fish. Justin wouldn't accept her offer to do it himself, so she'd just have to do it for him. Stubborn man!

It was slow going. The fish may have been growing tired, but it was far from docile. For every foot she gained, Ashley was sure she gave up two. Finally it came down to a battle of wills. Man, or woman in this case, against nature. With Justin's guidance, she eventually managed to get the monster fish close enough to the boat for him to use the net.

As Justin worked quickly and carefully to remove the hook from the fish, Ashley sat back in her chair, sure her arms would be numb for the rest of her life. Still breathing hard, she watched as Justin lifted the fish from the net and gently placed it in the livewell.

"Is he the one you've been waiting for?" she asked.

"He's close." Justin moved to the back of the boat and secured his gear. "Get your things put away. We're going in."

She did as instructed and then dropped into the passenger seat. When Justin climbed behind the wheel, she reached out and touched his arm, drawing his gaze.

"I'm sorry," she said. "I know how badly you wanted to catch him."

"It's a game of chance, Ashley. The fish was hungry and got to your bait first."

"As far as I'm concerned he can be your catch," she offered impulsively.

His eyes narrowed slightly as he stared at her. Ashley held his gaze, wishing she could read his mind. Finally a wry smile appeared and he shook his head.

"Thanks for the offer, but I think we better keep things honest."

Turning away, he switched on the engine and carefully maneuvered the boat out of the cove. When he hit open water, he shifted to full throttle and sent the boat skimming over the water at top speed.

Intrigued, Ashley watched as Justin docked the boat at the marina and sprinted along the boardwalk and up the incline to the office. The resulting flurry of activity was fascinating to witness.

She stood to the side as the fish was gently removed from the livewell and placed in a large cooler filled with lake water. It was then transferred, with all the care of a nuclear bomb, to the office where it was carefully weighed and measured. The atmosphere pulsed with excitement as everyone tried to talk at once. Phone calls were made, people came and went, and came back again.

Ashley took it all in as she sat at one of the tables in the adjoining restaurant, sipping a canned cola and munching on M&Ms. Judging by the uproar, her hunch must have been correct. The fish was a record catch and obviously a big deal to this crowd. Personally, she'd been more excited about the first fish she'd caught. Sure, it was big and had put up a hell of a fight, but so what? Cooked up in a skillet she didn't figure it would taste any better or worse than the others she'd had.

Justin seemed totally oblivious to her presence. She took the opportunity to study him as he asked questions, answered questions, and took telephone calls. It was interesting just to sit back and quietly have her visual fill of him. She liked the way he stood sometimes with his fingers tucked into the back pockets of his jeans and his legs braced apart. He was built solid, wide in the shoulders and narrow in the hips, like a man used to physical activity. He moved with an easy assurance and spoke with a quiet authority.

Just for the fun of it she tried to picture him in the type of clothing he'd be expected to wear if he'd stayed with the family business. It was nearly impossible to do. She had a hard time picturing him in a tailored suit or designer clothes since he looked so at home in jeans, a sweatshirt, and work boots. Even the unruliness of his jet black hair curling over his collar seemed more suitable for him than a neat haircut. She wondered absently if the same dark hair could be found on his chest.

Her wandering thoughts came to an abrupt halt when the door to the office flew open and a tall, heavyset man came charging into the room.

"Where is it?" he bellowed, his voice probably carrying halfway across the lake.

Someone directed him toward the cooler, and he walked over to peer into the open container. For a long moment he didn't move, just continued to stare as if witnessing a miracle straight from heaven.

"Well, I'll be damned," he declared. With a shake of his head, he turned and walked to Justin. He granted the younger man a vigorous handshake and a congratulatory slap on the shoulder.

"How much does it weigh?" he asked.

"Twelve pounds two ounces."

The old man gave a hoot of laughter. "Man, that's some fish. Now you got to tell us what it was like catching him."

Justin didn't answer immediately, and Ashley became aware of the sudden hush that settled over the room. Everyone's attention focused on Justin, waiting to hear the details of how he'd managed to land the new record smallmouth bass.

He turned, and his gaze locked with hers. In that instant she realized that he'd been aware all along of where she sat. She wondered at the indecision she saw in his eyes. Then he smiled as he lifted a hand toward her.

"I didn't catch the fish," he announced. "The lady in the back did."

* * *

Ashley dipped a fat french fry into a glob of catsup and popped it into her mouth. Chewing thoughtfully, she looked out the restaurant window and over the marina grounds. A long hedge of forsythia had bloomed into an explosion of color just outside the window. The late afternoon sun made the golden color seem even brighter.

Wondering what time it was, she turned to look over her shoulder at the restaurant clock. She saw that it was just after five. She also saw that more than a few curious glances were directed her way.

She turned back to her meal. "This has been a really crazy day," she remarked.

Justin gave a short laugh and leaned back in his chair. He braced one booted foot on the chair beside him and hooked his arm around the back of his own. "You've just made history. What do you expect?"

She rolled her eyes. "Why didn't you tell everyone you caught the fish?"

"Because I didn't."

The edge in his voice caught her attention. She regarded him a long moment before speaking. "It should have been your catch."

Something stirred in his eyes, something she didn't recognize and couldn't give a name to. A lazy smile appeared on his face. "You really bruised my ego today," he said, referring to the conversation they'd had a few days ago.

"You told me you could handle it. That it doesn't bother you."

"That was when it was just between you and me. Now you've gone and shown me up in front of the whole town. Probably the whole state before it's over. Maybe even the whole country."

"Oh, that's nonsense. Why would anyone outside of this area care about that fish?"

He straightened and leaned toward her. "Listen to me, Ashley. There are some things you need to understand—"

"Hey, Justin!" someone called out from across the restaurant.

Ashley and Justin both looked up to see a lanky man with frizzy blond hair and wire-rimmed glasses hurrying toward their table.

She was surprised to hear Justin swear softly. "You're about to meet Denny Whiteside, Windsong's local ace reporter."

"I'm glad I found you," Denny stated breathlessly as he pulled out the chair next to Justin and moved it around to the end of the table so that he could sit facing the two of them. He dropped into it and opened his notebook.

"Go ahead and join us, Denny." Barely concealed sarcasm tinged Justin's voice, giving the impression that he was less than thrilled by Denny's intrusion.

"Thanks." Denny turned sharp blue eyes to Ashley and stuck out his hand. "Hi. I'm Denny Whiteside, reporter for the Windsong Weekly. You must be Ashley Harper."

"That's me." She was amazed that such a scrawny fellow would have such a firm handshake.

"Can I ask you some questions?"

"Sure." Ashley went back to work on the few fries left on her plate. "Shoot away."

"Where are you from?"

"Knoxville. Born and raised there."

"And how long have you been an avid fisherman?"

Ashley looked at the Jimmy Olsen of Windsong and arched a brow. "I prefer the term angler," she responded coolly.

Denny's answering smile was just short of condescending. "Pardon me. How long have you been an avid *angler*?"

Ashley eyed him a moment before saying, "Let me think." She studied the tip of a french fry as if expecting to find the answer written there. "I have been an avid angler for . . ." She paused and lifted her gaze to Justin. "Six days, isn't it?"

He crossed his arms over his chest and nodded.

Her gaze flicked back to Denny. "Six days."

He began to write and then stopped. "Six days?" he repeated blankly.

"That's right. I picked up my first fishing pole last Saturday morning. This is Thursday. By my calculations that makes it six days."

Denny turned to Justin as if seeking confirmation of her answer.

"Write it down, Denny. Six days."

Denny scowled as he scribbled a note on his pad. Pursing his lips, he sat thoughtfully for a full minute before turning his attention back to Ashley. "How big was the fish you caught this morning, Miss Harper?"

She turned to Justin. "How big was Beauregard?"

"Beauregard?" Both men spoke in unison.

"I've decided to name the fish Beauregard," she explained calmly. "After all, if he's going to be famous, he needs a name to distinguish him from all the other smallmouth bass out there. Beauregard seems to me to be a nice solid name for a fish of his status. Don't you think?" She directed the question to Justin.

For a moment he simply stared at her. Then slowly, he nodded. "Beauregard weighed twelve pounds and two ounces."

Denny scribbled again, hesitated, looked from Ashley to Justin and then back to Ashley. "Are you planning to have him mounted?"

"No!" Ashley looked at Justin. "We don't have to do that, do we?"

"No. The Tennessee Wildlife Resources Agency will find a good home for him."

Relief flooded her. "Good."

"Are you two playing some kind of joke?" Denny demanded.

Ashley arched a brow. "Are you suggesting, Mr. Whiteside, that we're lying to you?"

"I'm suggesting that there's more to this story than what you're telling me."

"Is it so unbelievable that a mere woman, a novice angler, could have caught that fish?" Ashley challenged. "Let me assure you that Beauregard was my catch."

Denny looked at Justin. "You didn't help at all?"

"I netted him."

"Mr. Whiteside, let me explain this to you," Ashley

started patiently. "I put a very pretty blue lure on the end of my hook and threw it into the water. I can't tell you the name of the lure or the name of the fishing pole, for that matter. I used whatever Justin gave me to use. If you want details, you'll have to ask him. If you want to know why the fish took my bait, then I can't help you. Chalk it up to beginner's luck." She pushed her chair back and stood. "Now, if you'll excuse me, I'd really like to call it a day."

Chapter Six

"I just don't understand what all the uproar is about," Ashley said for the third time since they'd started home from the marina. She slammed the door to the Blazer and walked around it to face Justin. "It's a stupid fish, for heaven's sake. For all the attention I'm getting, you'd think I'd walked on water today instead of pulled a fish out of it."

For the third time, Justin tried to explain. "Listen to me, Ashley. This isn't just a hobby. Fishing is a big business and something like what happened today is going to bring out a lot of interested people. You've hit the jackpot here, whether you believe it or not. Everything has been documented. The type of rod and reel you were using, the lure, the fishing line, the boat you were in. Everything. Some of those companies are going to be willing to pay you to tell your story and promote the part their product played in your success."

"But I don't want any of that!" Her adamant protest echoed in the still night. "It's all your stuff, Justin. They should come to you for that information. I don't know about any of those things. I can't promote anything. I don't *know* anything." She nearly cringed at the note of panic in her voice.

Frowning, Justin stared at her. "You know, Ashley, I don't understand you. You love to try new things. Nick told me you went skydiving a couple of years ago. Scared him to death, but you loved it. Yet the thought of what could happen because of a stroke of luck today throws you into a complete panic. Can you explain that to me?"

"Yes," she answered immediately. "When I decide to try something, I'm making the conscious decision to do so. I do my research, plot my strategy, and go from there. I'm in control."

"No, you're not. You have no control when you jump out of an airplane and depend on a thin piece of fabric to open and keep you from becoming a broken mess on the ground."

"But the odds of a chute not opening are minimal. I knew that going in."

"Well, the odds of you catching that fish today were astronomical, but it didn't keep it from happening, did it?"

She kicked at a rock in the driveway. "It should have been your catch."

"Damn right it should have been. Fate's having a good laugh right now, I'm sure."

She peered at him closely. "You *are* angry about not catching the fish. I knew it."

"Ah, hell." He slashed a hand through his hair and let out a heavy breath. "Let's don't move all this to a personal level. We've got enough trouble there as it is. Let's just figure out how we're going to solve the immediate problem facing us."

They stared at one another a long moment. Ashley felt an almost overwhelming urge to go to him. Just for a moment. Just to feel the warmth of his arms around her. Just to lean on his strength for a little while.

Then she realized she couldn't lean on someone she'd already pushed away.

Turning, she walked to the porch and dropped down to sit on the top step. Wearily, she ran her hands over her face. She was tired and confused. All she wanted was to go to sleep and wake up in the morning to discover this had all been a fantastic dream. There was no record smallmouth bass and there was no Justin Holmes.

She looked over to where he stood, his back to her, his hands tucked into the back pockets of his jeans. Did she really want to wish him away? Or did she want to wish away the barriers that kept her from accepting what she sensed he could give her?

"Will you help me?" she asked quietly.

He turned and started toward her. "Help you how?"

She shrugged. "I don't know exactly. Just be with me. Help me field the questions. Help me decide which offers are good and which ones aren't." She shrugged again. "Just stay with me."

"All you have to do is tell your story, smile pretty for the camera, and accept the money offered you. It's really not much more complicated than that."

"It is for me. I don't like surprises and this trip has been full of them. I like things planned out and road maps carefully drawn up."

He crouched in front of her. "Haven't you noticed yet that life is full of surprises? Some good. Some bad. Life isn't meant to be controlled. It's meant to be enjoyed."

"I've always been so busy trying to control things that I never leaned how to enjoy things much," she admitted ruefully.

"You've just described the main reason I walked away from my father and the family business. From the day I was born and given the name Justin Thomas Holmes, Junior, my life was completely mapped out for me. No one ever asked me what I wanted to be. No one ever considered that I might want something different than being CEO of Holmes Enterprises. As J.T.'s oldest son, I was expected to follow in his footsteps."

"It must have been hard for you growing up. Is that why you ran away that summer?"

He nodded and shifted to sit beside her on the step. "I was an angry young man by that point, already being groomed to take over the mighty corporation." He gave a sardonic laugh. "All I wanted was to play baseball. I had a chance to go to a summer camp to work on my pitching.

I was so excited I could hardly stand it. But my father had other, more important, plans. He'd arranged for me to travel with him that summer to all of the branch companies of Holmes Enterprises. We were going to travel all over the world. What was a baseball summer camp compared to that, he'd reasoned.'' Justin looked at her. "To a fourteen-year-old baseball fanatic, it was like trading in heaven for hell."

"So you took off?"

"Yeah." He turned to stare out into the darkness. "When you're that age and that angry, you have no fear. I thumbed my way from New York to Knoxville and never once thought about the danger of what I was doing. I intended to go all the way to L.A., figuring that was the farthest I could get from J.T. Holmes and all he stood for."

"What happened when you got to Knoxville?"

"A dark street on the wrong side of town and a group of boys angrier than me. Thanks to a man walking his two Dobermans, I was able to walk away from the incident under my own steam. I suspect I would have ended up dead if he hadn't come along when he did. He wanted to call the police, but for obvious reasons that was the last thing I wanted. I remembered Nick lived there and looked up his name in the phone book. He came right away and picked me up, no questions asked. Of course, later I realized J.T. had alerted him to my departure. I really thought he'd put me on the next direct flight to New York. But he didn't. He offered to let me stay. He squared it with my parents, and I spent the best summer of my life in Knoxville, Tennessee."

"I was only six that summer so I don't remember much. I knew Mom had gone away forever and Daddy was sad. That was why he wanted Sara and me to stay with our grandparents that summer."

"He was so lonely," Justin murmured. "We talked a lot, usually while we fished. I talked about my dreams, and for the first time in my life I knew someone was hearing what I was saying. Nick talked about Diane. I can remember thinking that I didn't ever want to love someone as much as he'd loved her. I didn't ever want to risk hurting as badly as he did."

He turned to look at her. "But I've learned something important since then." His voice dropped, becoming a caress, drawing out her emotions. "What your parents shared was so special that I'd give just about anything to find a love that strong and enduring. A love like theirs would be worth the risk."

The tears spilling over and tracing down Ashley's cheeks brought her no shame. She'd been too young to remember her parents together. Justin had just given her something priceless. Something she could tuck away in her heart with the faded memories and cherish in the years to come.

She felt his hands come up to gently frame her face. His thumbs smoothed the moisture from her skin, only to have it replaced by new tears. He bent and kissed her forehead, and then drew her into the shelter of his arms. She pressed her cheek against his chest, the steady beat of his heart a promise beneath her ear. No one but her father had ever held her when she'd cried. But she felt at home in Justin's arms. She didn't allow herself to debate the right or wrong of her feelings. All she wanted now was to enjoy the comfort she found with this man.

Justin's phone began to ring bright and early on Friday morning. One of the first calls came from the Honorable Henry Winston, the mayor of Windsong. He wanted to know if it would be convenient for Justin and Ashley to come into town for a special presentation at two that afternoon. He assured Justin that it would be nothing extravagant, just a little get-together of the townsfolk. After all, nothing this exciting had happened in Windsong since Nelson Smith had won all that money in the Kentucky lottery. Of course, when Nelson ran off with the preacher's daughter a week later, it put a bit of a taint on the good luck story.

Shortly before two, Justin pulled the Blazer onto Main Street and headed toward the town square. It was visibly apparent that the good citizens of Windsong had been very busy in the last twenty-four hours. American flags waved in the breeze, adding a truly patriotic air to the occasion. The storefronts and houses lining Main Street were spotless, the lawns all neatly trimmed. To anyone looking on, Windsong was a picture perfect town of Southern hospitality. And if the media trucks parked along the street were any indication, America would indeed be looking in on Windsong.

Justin found a parking spot on the grocery lot and shut off the engine. He looked over at Ashley and wondered what her thoughts were as she stared out the window. With the exception of the nervous movement of her hands in her lap, she appeared to be calm enough.

She wore a denim split skirt, tan leather boots, and a yellow short-sleeved sweater with a row of tiny pearl buttons down the front. She'd left her hair loose except for the two barrettes sweeping back the sides from her face. She looked very classy and not at all like the woman who had reeled in the record smallmouth bass only yesterday.

"You look great," he complimented.

She shot him a quick smile and smoothed her hands over the skirt. "Thanks. I really didn't expect to wear this. It was in one of those cases you had to lug to the truck that first day. You remember referring to my impractical wardrobe?"

He grinned . "I remember. Guess it wasn't so impractical after all." He reached for her hand and was pleased when she readily placed it in his. "Are you ready? We're late."

"I know." She looked back out the window. "Are all those television stations here for this?"

"Looks like it."

"I guess this is a bigger deal that I thought."

"Come on. You're going to be fine." He released her hand and climbed out of the truck. He'd traded his usual attire for gray twill trousers and a solid red polo shirt. When he came around to her side, she was already out and waiting. She pulled a small bag of M&Ms out of her pocket and shook a few into her palm before popping them into her mouth.

"Do you go anywhere without those?" he asked.

"No." She shrugged. "Some people smoke. Some people drink. I eat M&Ms."

He shook his head. "Let's go."

She reached for his hand this time. "You won't leave me?" she asked as they crossed the street and headed toward the town square.

"I won't leave you." It was a promise he thought he might be tempted to keep for a lifetime if she'd let him.

"I looked scared to death," Ashley grumbled as she turned off Justin's television following the broadcast of their afternoon interview.

"You looked great," Justin replied.

"I sounded stupid." She dropped into the large recliner and reached down to scratch Dudley's head. "Why didn't you just tell everyone you caught the stupid fish and save me from all this?"

Justin sighed and stood. "You did fine. Quit being so critical of yourself."

She closed her eyes and leaned back in the chair. "I want to go home and put all this behind me."

He paused beside her. "This won't end when you leave here, Ashley." He gestured toward a message pad beside his phone. "I've got a list of people over there who want to talk to you. It's not going to matter to them if they talk to you here, or if they talk to you in Knoxville."

"I don't have to talk to anybody," she retorted stubbornly, coming to her feet. "It's a free country, and I don't have to do anything I don't want to do. No one can dictate to me." She slashed a hand through the air. "Not you. Not them. No one!" She turned and rushed out of the cabin. The door slammed at the same instant the phone rang.

Justin swore softly before grabbing the receiver. "This is Justin Holmes."

"I'll bet you're wishing you had my head on a platter right about now."

Justin smiled, recognizing Nick's voice. "Actually, I started visualizing that about a week ago."

Soft laughter drifted through the telephone line. "I'm not surprised. I don't suppose you entertained any hopes of catching that fish."

"Never crossed my mind."

"Right. Will it help if I say I'm sorry?"

"Hell, no."

"I didn't think so."

Justin chuckled. "I seem to remember you telling me once that fishing was more about luck than skill. I think Ashley's proven that."

"I saw the two of you on the news. She looked pretty tense. Is she okay?"

Justin heard the fatherly concern in the other man's voice. "No, she's still pretty tense. She's not handling this very well at all."

"I didn't figure she would. How are you doing?"

"I'm pretty tense, too."

"Is she around there anywhere?"

Justin reached up to rub the back of his neck. "She just stormed out of her a minute ago. I can hear music drifting through the air, so she must have gone back to her cabin."

"Does she have any M&Ms?"

Justin had to laugh. "I'm sure she does. She doesn't ever seem to be without."

"Good. She'll be fine then."

"I think she's addicted to those things."

"No doubt. But I quit worrying about it years ago figuring there are worst things to be addicted to."

"I won't argue with that." Justin paused a moment. "Things are going to be crazy for awhile, Nick. Are you going to be able to help her keep everything on an even keel?"

"I'll do what I can. But I'm in the middle of a big case that's keeping me pretty busy. I won't have as much time as I'd like."

"What about her fiancé?"

A heavy silence followed the question. "What fiancé?" Nick asked slowly.

Hearing the guarded edge in his friend's voice, Justin

hesitated. "I thought she was engaged to a guy named Anderson."

"I hope to God not! If she's gone and . . . Did she tell you she was engaged?"

"Yeah, on several occasions," Justin returned dryly.

"Oh, Lord. She doesn't have a ring on, does she?"

The concern in Nick's voice intrigued Justin. "No, there isn't a ring. She says they've been too busy to get one."

"Right. Geoffrey Anderson's been too busy, that's for sure. I don't trust the man. I can't figure out why Ashley is even attracted to him."

"Well, I can't answer that. All I know is what she's told me."

"I know." Nick sighed again. "None of this is your problem anyway, Justin. We'll work things out when Ashley gets home. Thanks for all you've done."

"I haven't done much of anything. By the way, that extra check you sent with Ashley is in tiny pieces in the trash. I won't take your money, Nick, you know that."

"You deserve to be paid—"

"I've been paid. Nice talking to you."

"Justin—"

Grinning, Justin cut the connection.

Justin sat on the porch swing, watching the day slip away. As the sun dipped behind the trees and the shadows lengthened, a refreshing chill filled the air. Nearby, the melancholy call of a bobwhite echoed in the stillness. A few seconds later an answer came in the distance.

These tranquil moments suspended between daylight and darkness brought a sense of peace to Justin. It was at this time of day that he was most certain he'd made the right decision to leave New York eight years ago. Now he wondered if his days of living in obscurity were numbered.

He figured it would only be a matter of time before some enterprising reporter made the connection between himself and J.T. And he knew from past experience that the discovery would be played up as a big deal. After all, he was heir to a fortune and wealthy even without his father's money.

Sitting there in the deepening solitude, Justin could almost hear the speculations being voiced. What right did he have to pass himself off as a simple fishing guide? With the kind of money he had, he could go anywhere and do anything. Why would he waste his time in a little Tennessee town?

Few people would understand his choice to be here. Fewer would even try.

Dudley lifted his head and looked toward the drive, his eyes and ears alert. A moment later Ashley stepped into view, her hands pushed deep into the pockets of her skirt, her head bent slightly as she walked. Justin watched her approach the cabin. She wasn't aware of his presence on the porch until she started to climb the steps.

She stopped to look at him, her expression pensive. "I'm sorry about earlier," she offered quietly.

He held her gaze, keeping the surprise he felt to himself. "There's no need. I know this isn't easy for you."

She leaned back against the railing, her hands working nervously inside her pockets. "No, it isn't. But that doesn't give me the right to take my frustrations out on you. I know you're only trying to help me."

"You don't make it easy."

"I know. It's because you scare me."

He studied her a moment before shaking his head. "It's not me you're scared of, Ashley. It's yourself. Why don't you be honest about that at least."

He saw the anger flare in her eyes and smolder there as she glared at him. Just as quickly it disappeared as her lids drifted shut and she sighed deeply. "You want honesty, Justin?" Her eyes opened and she met his gaze directly. "A week ago I had my life all planned out. I thought I knew exactly what I wanted and how I was going to go about getting it. Now everything is slightly out of focus. Everything that seemed so clear, doesn't make perfect sense anymore. And I'm not even sure why."

"Tell me what's changed for you."

She took a deep breath and turned to look out into the

shadows. "I never enjoyed being out like this. I always thought I thrived on the constant activity of the city. Now I'm not so sure." She shook her head. "I've come to enjoy the beauty and the solitude here. I like hearing the birds early in the morning and the mysterious sounds of the night. I like the wind whispering through the trees and the rain hitting the roof. I never noticed those things in the city. This morning I saw a deer in the clearing. I've never seen anything like that before, and I really believed it didn't matter." She turned to look over her shoulder at him. "But for some reason, now it does."

"A lot of people come out here and are won over by the solitude and beauty they find. They may not be consciously looking for it, but they find it just the same. You're not so unusual, Ashley."

"But there's more. I've never believed in romantic love. Maybe if my mother had lived, if I could have seen the love you say she and Daddy shared, then maybe I'd know what to look for. I think I see it in Cal and Jessi. But it's not anything I can pinpoint, it's just a sense of emotion so strong I can't even give it a name." She shrugged, trying to express something she didn't fully understand. "And Angie stirs more feelings that I don't recognize. I never thought I wanted children until I watched Jessi and Angie. Now I just don't know for sure." She gave a sharp laugh and slipped her hands back into her pockets. "And on top of all that I have to contend with an overgrown fish . . . and you."

Justin stood and slowly crossed the porch to stand beside her. "You've already made it clear how you feel about me."

"Have I? I'm afraid you'll hurt me," she admitted, her heart in her eyes. "I'm afraid it's all a trick, some kind of magic that won't last beyond these woods."

"Ashley, you're looking for guarantees that don't exist. Much of what we feel for one another right now is simple desire. At this point I don't know what's beyond that. I'm experiencing some new emotions, too. I thought I'd be content to spend the rest of my life right here. Alone. I didn't realize I was lonely until you came." He brushed his knuckles down her cheek. "I'm not looking for an affair, and I don't ever want to hurt you. But I can't map out the future for you. No one can.''

She caught his hand in hers. With her gaze locked on his, she pressed a kiss to his open palm. The impact of the simple gesture slammed into him with the force of an ocean wave at high tide. His need for her was instantaneous and strong. How easy it would be to sweep her into his arms and away from all her doubts and fears. They could have this one night apart from all the questions and complications. Just one night.

He bent toward her, his hands sliding beneath the hair at the back of her neck. She slipped into his embrace willingly, tilting her head back so that his mouth had no trouble finding hers. He heard her soft sigh of pleasure as her lips parted and he deepened the kiss. Her body, soft and pliable, pressed intimately against the tautness of his own. After a long moment, he drew back slightly to look down into her face.

Her eyes were closed, but her hands moved restlessly up and down his back. He bent to her again, raining adoring kisses on each of her features. His fingers slipped through the silky strands of her hair before gathering it together into one fist. Gently, he tugged, tilting her head back further.

Her eyes opened to stare into his, and he saw the passionate glaze in their dark depths. A sensuous smile bloomed, first curving her lips and then lighting her eyes. He felt her hands urging him closer and did nothing to resist. Her kiss was hot and hungry, designed to further weaken him. He wrapped his arms around her and let himself sink into the sensations she created.

Ashley felt the world spinning around her, knew she had no control, and didn't even care. She tunneled her hands beneath Justin's shirt, compelled by the need to touch him. She ran her palms up the solid length of his back and brought them back down, raking her nails gently over his warm skin. She felt him tremble just before he lifted her into his arms. Wrapping her arms around his neck, she buried her face against his shoulder, trusting herself to him in a way she'd never trusted herself to anyone before. She pushed all her doubts away, unwilling to let them taint this perfect moment in time.

A seductive twilight shrouded them as he carried her to his bedroom. A soft breeze drifted through the open windows, bringing with it the scent of the outdoors. Gently, he lowered her to the middle of the big bed and sat down next to her. With patient fingers he began to release each of the tiny buttons running the length of her sweater.

His gaze never wavered from hers, and Ashley found herself mesmerized by the promise in his blue eyes. She could feel her heart pick up its rhythm each time his fingers brushed the flesh beneath the sweater. When the last button was free, cool air trailed across her heated skin as he peeled the garment away. Her lacy bra followed the sweater.

Ashley felt a tightening in the pit of her stomach as he bent toward her and buried his face against her neck. She arched her head away, allowing him better access as he traced a line of kisses down her shoulder. His hand came to rest on her waist, then slowly slid upward. Her body tensed with anticipation as his hand cupped the underside of her breast and his mouth closed over the peak.

Something snapped inside her, surprising her, causing her to cry out in the stillness. It was a temporary release, leaving her nerve endings even more sensitive to his touch. Justin continued to work magic with his hands and mouth, taking her on a roller coaster ride of sensation.

When he finally kissed his way back up to her mouth, she pulled him close, wanting to feel the length of him against her. Her hands worked to push his shirt up. He drew away from her and pulled it over his head, tossing it to the side.

She found the mat of dark hair covering his chest soft beneath her palms. When her fingers brushed his nipples, she heard his sharp intake of breath. Looking up into his face, she watched, fascinated, as she came back to touch the sensitive area. His eyes closed, and his breathing took on a harsh edge as the flesh beneath her fingers hardened.

Feeling a surge of excitement at her ability to arouse him so, she leaned into him, replacing the play of her fingers with her lips. His hand cupped the back of her head, briefly holding her to him, before he groaned deep in his throat and pushed her back onto the mattress. He followed her down, his mouth claiming hers in an explosion of heat. Her arms snaked around him, sliding downward until her hands rested on his hips. The roughness of his trousers chafed her hands after the smoothness of his skin. Instinctively, she arched against him, transmitting without words her desire.

She was caught in a red haze of sensual feeling that was completely foreign to her. She'd never felt anything like this—ever. Justin's touch bewitched her, drew her deeper into the erotic, silken web he'd created just for her. She was helpless to break the spell he'd cast, her body reacting spontaneously to his touch. His hands played her, teased her, yet never quite made the intimate contact she yearned for. All she could do was wait while the ache she felt deep inside grew and intensified with each caress.

"Make love to me," she whispered as her fingers slipped down to work at his belt buckle. "I want you. I want to feel all of you."

He pulled away from her and reached down to capture her hands. Gently, he drew them up over her head, holding them there with one hand as his other tenderly caressed her cheek. "We can't make love, Ashley."

She stared at him, confused by this turn of events. "But—"

"I want to," he assured her, "more than I want to breathe. But I'm not prepared, and I won't risk you getting pregnant."

Before she could protest further, he kissed her again, pulling her back into the sensual fog and away from the reality of his words. He stroked his fingers lightly over her breast and downward to the waistband of her skirt. He trailed his lips across her cheek to her ear where he whispered, "I can still love you, Ashley."

A shudder raced through her body as he released the button and lowered the zipper of her skirt.

Chapter Seven

Ashley opened her eyes, slowly taking in her surroundings as the events of the previous evening filtered through her mind. She was alone in the bed, still wrapped in the cocoonlike warmth of the thick comforter. She remembered falling asleep in Justin's arms. She didn't remember him leaving her.

She pushed a tangle of hair back from her face and rolled onto her back. For the first time she noticed the twin skylights in the ceiling. Sunlight danced through the trees, casting patterns of light upon the bed. She raised up on an elbow and looked around the room. The door was shut and she was alone. Lying neatly at the foot of the bed were a pair of her jeans, a blue cotton camp shirt, and underwear. Her clothes from the day before were folded and stacked neatly on the dresser.

She drew in a deep breath and slipped from the bed. As she showered, she tried to analyze her feelings. They were ambiguous at best. She couldn't ignore the fact that she'd never felt more cherished than she had the night before. The memory caused her skin to heat. Justin had given her something precious, something rare. But despite the beauty of what she'd experienced, she wasn't sure it had changed anything for her.

She turned her face to the cool spray of the shower and let it flow over her. Did she dare hope that this flame of desire between her and Justin could be real? Could it last? Or would it fizzle out over time, leaving them with nothing more than memories of what used to be?

He'd told her there were no guarantees. Of course he was right. But wasn't that why it was wiser to make a decision based on something other than fickle emotions? She thought of Geoffrey. Life with him would be dependable. Solid. She doubted that there would be many surprises with him.

With Justin she was afraid there would be too many surprises.

She turned off the water, wondering why she'd allowed things to get so complicated. A week ago she'd known where she was going and how she planned to get there. Why had she allowed a stranger with captivating blue eyes and a love for children and dogs to turn her world upside-down?

As she shrugged into her shirt, she caught a glimpse of herself in the mirror over the vanity. She paused and stared at the familiar reflection. Had she changed? Physically, she looked the same, but she felt different.

Justin had opened a whole new world to her. She couldn't see it clearly, but the temptation she felt to explore it further tugged at her. What more could he show her, teach her? How far was she willing to trust him? She thought of his unselfish loving of the night before and knew, without a doubt, that she could trust him completely.

In that instant Ashley faced her greatest fear. She was a heartbeat away from falling head-over-heels in love with Justin Holmes. The thought overwhelmed her while the intensity of her feelings for him terrified her. She had no idea what to do next.

Justin was talking on the phone when Ashley walked out of the bedroom. Their eyes met briefly, holding for a moment, before he turned away, intent on his conversation. She placed her bundle of clothes on a chair and went into the kitchen to pour herself a cup of coffee. Taking the steaming brew with her, she stepped out into the fresh morning. Dudley sat on the top step of the porch, his tail wagging in greeting. Ashley gave him a friendly pat as she sat beside him.

She enjoyed the sunny solitude for a few moments before Justin came out onto the porch. He didn't join her on the step, even though there was plenty of room. He went instead to lean against the railing.

Ashley felt incredibly nervous, which seemed ridiculous considering what had transpired between them. But she couldn't help it. What did you say to the man who had only a few hours earlier intimately explored your body and given such intense pleasure?

"Good morning." His firm, quiet voice broke into her chaotic thoughts.

She returned the greeting, but didn't turn to him.

She heard him shift and move. And then he was crouching beside her, his fingers capturing her chin and tilting it up. With his other hand he took her coffee cup and set it aside. Her gaze flew up to meet his, and the heat in those incredible eyes sliced straight through her. He smiled as he leaned forward and kissed her.

Even though she knew she was sitting on a solid structure, she still felt as if she might slide right off the face of the earth. She reached for him, her fingers digging into his forearms. And then she didn't care how fast the world spun as long as he controlled the speed.

Justin felt her surrender and his own self-control nearly snap. He was playing with fire, acknowledged the fact, and deepened the kiss. He'd lived thirty-five years, played at love a few times, and had never even come close to what he felt for Ashley.

The full force of his feelings had hit him sometime around dawn when he'd awakened with her warm body curled next to his. There, in the first dim light of a new day, he took the final step off the deep end. A deluge of emotions had swamped his senses. Desire, sharp and edgy, had led the way, and it had taken every ounce of willpower he possessed to suppress his need to lose himself in her. Leaving her alone in his bed had been the toughest test of self-discipline he'd ever survived.

Her arms slipped around his waist now, and he moved to balance himself on his knees. His hands slid into her hair, the damp strands gliding through his fingers like silk. After a moment, he drew away from her, his hands still in her hair, and looked down into her face. Her skin was flushed and a secret smile curved her lips as a soft sigh whispered across them. Dark eyes, clouded by emotion, looked up into his.

Mesmerized was the word that popped into his head. How easily he could mesmerize her. But being mesmerized was not the same as being in love.

"You have a unique way of saying good morning," she murmured, her hands moving lightly up and down his back.

"Oh, but I can do much better. If you stick around long enough, I'll show you."

He saw the lazy pleasure warm her eyes. But he knew the instant reality worked its way into her thoughts. The warmth cooled, degree by degree, until there was none. Her arms dropped from his waist and she stood.

He let her go without comment and pushed to his feet. In a heartbeat he knew she wouldn't be staying any longer than her original plans. Despite what he made her feel, despite every indication of what could develop between them, she wasn't going to alter her carefully mapped out life.

At least now he knew. The knowledge didn't ease the pain, but he could do himself the favor of facing the truth head-on.

As she moved to the far end of the porch, he leaned back against the railing and crossed one leg over the other at the ankles. He adopted the casual pose hoping to steady his own nerves.

"I just had a phone conversation I think you'll find interesting," he said.

She hesitated slightly before turning to face him. "With whom?"

"A representative from a company called Still Waters. They manufacture a line of fishing gear, including the lure you were using when you caught Beauregard. For the last five years they've been offering a cash award for the person who caught the new record smallmouth bass, if that person was using one of their lures." He smiled. "The gentleman I talked to would like to come down early in the week and verify your catch."

She shook her head and looked out over the sun-drenched yard. "I have to get back to work, Justin."

"Don't you want to know how much that pretty blue lure is worth?"

She looked over at him and shrugged. "I guess. How much?"

"How about two hundred thousand dollars?"

Her mouth opened, but nothing came out. She stared at him, clearly stunned.

He laughed softly. "In Vegas they call this hitting the jackpot."

"My God. You must have misunderstood."

"No. I've seen the ads myself in several fishing magazines. I called yesterday to make sure they were aware of the catch. They're anxious to meet you."

She shook her head again as she reached out to grasp the railing and steady herself. "I can't take that money, Justin. You deserve it. It was your lure."

"You caught the fish. We've already been over this issue."

"But it's not fair to you. I won't take it."

"I don't want your money, Ashley. Give it away if you want. Just don't try to give it to me."

She turned abruptly and paced the width of the porch. "What kind of company would make that kind of offer? I mean, that much money for a fish? Does that make any sense?"

"You're the only person I know who'd complain about a windfall of two hundred thousand dollars."

"This whole thing is so silly. I can't quite grasp it."

He straightened and slid his hands into his jeans pockets. "Well, let me give you some friendly advice. Don't let anyone hear you complain about the money. You can let it sit in the bank, you can give it away to your favorite charity, or you can buy a warehouse full of M&Ms. Just remember that no one is going to have much sympathy for what you perceive as a problem."

She tucked a strand of hair behind her ear and took a deep breath. "I see your point." A sudden, mischievous light came into her eyes, followed by a smile. "Will you at least let me buy you an expensive dinner sometime?"

"I might." He was amazed he even had a voice to answer. With just one playful look, he felt as if someone had planted a well-aimed punch to his solar plexus. He wondered if she had any idea how potent her charm was. Then he wondered how he was supposed to deal with it.

"I'll hold you to it," she promised.

He turned away, needing to do something before the temptation to drag her into his arms and carry her inside became stronger than his will. He bent and picked up her coffee cup.

"I've got some errands to run today," he said. "Care to tag along?"

She hesitated, then shook her head. "I better not," she said, walking over to the steps. "I've got to get my packing done if we're going to spend tomorrow at Jessi's."

He nodded. "Then I guess I'll see you later."

"Yeah, I guess so." She gazed up at him a moment before hurrying away.

Justin let out the breath he'd been holding. He shut down hard on the disappointment threatening to overtake him. He'd seen indecision in her eyes and had hoped—

Abruptly he swore and carried the cup into the house. She was going back to where she belonged. He was a bigger risk than she was willing to take. Her decision hadn't come as a surprise. The real surprise came from knowing how lonely his life was going to be without her in it.

* * *

Ashley stood inside the screened front door of the Miles's farmhouse, undetected by the group on the front lawn. Someone had produced a Nerf football and play was underway. Of course, Justin was in the thick of it. It appeared that his team consisted of all the kids under the age of twelve. At one point Ashley had counted at least fifteen team members. Cal's team, on the other hand, consisted of four other adults and a handful of teenagers. It made for an interesting match-up.

Voices and laughter drifted into the house. A lot of that laughter came from Justin. He seemed to be most relaxed when in the company of children. She wondered if he was trying to gain back some of the childhood he'd been denied. If so, he appeared to be succeeding.

A hand touched her shoulder, and Ashley looked over as Jessi joined her.

"Looks like Justin's got the winning team," Jessi remarked. "Those little ones are sneaky."

Ashley laughed softly. "So is Justin."

"Is Angie out there?" Jessi's gaze swept the playing area.

"They decided she wasn't quite big enough to get into the fray. Justin and Cal sold her on the idea of being the cheerleader." Ashley pointed across the yard. "See her over there with Aunt Lila?"

"Good. She's out of harm's way."

"I've never known a place with so much laughter and love," Ashley said, reflecting on the scene outside.

"That's what we specialize in. I'm glad you came, Ashley."

The two women exchanged a smile. "I'm going to miss this," Ashley admitted.

"No one said you couldn't come back. You're welcome anytime. I've already told you that."

"I know." Ashley turned back to look out the door. "I just have a strange feeling that once I leave, I may never be able to come back."

She felt Jessi's curious gaze, but didn't turn to meet it. She didn't know how to explain what she'd just said.

Something kept nagging at her. Windsong was far removed from the life she lived in Knoxville. And once she got back to that life, this week would drift away like smoke on the breeze until it became nothing more than a pleasant memory.

She felt a hot ache of emotion, suddenly wanting more than anything the power to freeze time at just this precise point and never move on. She wanted to continue to share in the love found on this Tennessee farm. Maybe what she really wanted was the love of the man who was swinging a squealing Angie high into the air. The same man who had taken her to mysterious and delirious heights two nights ago.

Tears stung the back of her eyes, and she turned away from the door, unable to watch any longer.

"What is it, Ashley?" Jessi asked, her voice tinged with concern.

"You know what I'd like to do before I go?" Ashley said, hoping to cover her raw emotions and change the subject at the same time. "I'd like to see some of your work. Can we do that now?"

Jessi wasn't easily fooled. She studied Ashley a long moment, her green eyes serious and uncertain. Then she smiled gently and lifted a hand toward the back stairs. "Now's as good a time as any."

She led the way down the narrow staircase and turned on the light switch at the bottom. Low hanging shop lights chased away the shadows. Floor to ceiling metal shelves lined two walls, providing storage for everything from plaster molds to paints and glazes. A large table sat in the center of the room, its surface covered with projects in various stages of completion.

"This is where I work," Jessi explained. "The kiln is in the back. Cal enclosed it so it would be away from my work area."

"You have quite a set-up here." Ashley looked around the room. The quality of Jessi's supplies indicated she was very serious about her craft. Various projects were scattered across the worktable. A half-painted figurine off to the side caught Ashley's attention and she reached to pick it up.

She judged it to be about four inches tall. The ceramic felt smooth in her hands as she examined the exquisite craftsmanship. She immediately identified the piece as a grandmother. Jessi had already painted the hair white and the apron a blue-and-white gingham check. The happy smile on the figurine's face produced plump cheeks and eyes crinkled with laughter. The love radiating from the face was almost tangible.

"What color will her dress be?" Ashley asked thoughtfully.

"Red. Her shoes will be white and her eyes will be blue."

"She's lovely. The detail work is incredible."

"Thank you. She's part of a family set."

Ashley looked up. "Do you have others done?"

"Sure." Jessi crossed the room and pulled open the doors of a large cabinet. Ashley followed, her eyes widening at the sight of two deep shelves filled with small figures. Everything from babies to frail grandpas, each expression minutely detailed.

"Oh, Jessi," she whispered. "These are fantastic."

"Thanks. They're my design. I call them Family Folks."

Ashley's interest sharpened. She picked up another grandmother, only this one had brown hair and brown eyes. The next one had blond hair. Some were plump, some thin, but they were all unmistakably the same figure.

"My idea," Jessi explained, "is that anyone can build their own collection of figurines based on their own family unit." She reached for the figure of a man with dark hair. "This could be Cal." She picked out a little girl with red curls. "Here's Angie. And this . . ." She plucked a young woman with red hair from the back of the shelf. "This is me. I've now completed my whole family."

"What a unique idea. Have you sold many of these?"

"Just around here at craft fairs and bazaars. I've had quite a few orders for specific pieces. People seem to like them."

Ashley picked up a small boy and studied it. As all the others, it was perfectly done. "Would you be interested in setting up a display in my shop?"

There was a moment of suspended silence. "Are you serious?"

"We can do it as a kind of test market. We'll see how my customers feel about them."

"Oh, that would be wonderful." Jessi's excitement shone in her eyes. She reached out and impulsively hugged Ashley. "Thank you!"

Ashley laughed as she returned the hug. "You're welcome. Give me a couple of weeks to get all this business with the fish behind me, then we'll set up a time for you to come to the shop. Is that okay?"

"Wonderful," Jessi assured her, grinning.

"Jess?" Cal called from the top of the stairs.

"I'm right here."

"Is Ashley with you?"

"Yes."

Ashley walked to the bottom of the stairs and looked up at him.

"There's someone here to see you," he said. "Says his name is Anderson."

She felt a jolt of astonishment at Cal's announcement. What in the world was Geoffrey doing here? How had he found her?

Cal stepped back as she hurried up the stairs. "He's out front."

Ashley nodded and walked to the front door, pausing there to peer outside. Sure enough, Geoffrey stood there in the yard talking with Justin. He was dressed casually in a gray sports shirt and navy twill pants. Dark glasses shaded his eyes and the sun glinted off his neatly trimmed blond hair.

She hesitated, feeling a torrent of confusing emotions rush over her. This was the man she planned to spend the rest of her life with. Why didn't the sight of him stir more excitement in her?

Pushing the door open, she stepped out onto the porch. Justin's gaze swung immediately to her, capturing her eyes with his own. She couldn't decipher what was revealed in the blue depths, but she felt as if her soul had just been branded.

"Ashley, honey!" Geoffrey called, forcing her to refocus her attention on him. He started toward her, removing his sunglasses and slipping them into his shirt pocket.

She walked down the steps to meet him. "This is a surprise. What are you doing here?"

His hands spanned her waist in a possessive gesture. "Are you kidding? Once I heard the news I knew I had to come." His voice lowered. "You have to be careful now. People will try to take advantage of you."

Ashley frowned. "I don't think I understand."

"I'll explain it to you later." He shot her an indulgent smile as he drew her closer. "Come here and let me show you how much I've missed you."

He bent and pressed his lips to hers. She didn't move into the kiss or away, but merely accepted it. She had never felt a flare of emotion when Geoffrey kissed her, only a warm contentment. Now, oddly, she felt nothing at all.

If Geoffrey noticed any change, he didn't show it. He drew back from her and reached down for her hand. Gently, he began to lead her away from the boisterous crowd.

Ashley followed, aware every step of the way that they were being watched. She knew if she turned, she'd find Justin's gaze fixed squarely on her.

"How did you find me?" she asked.

"Oh, it wasn't hard. The people at the Starlight Marina told me I'd find you out here." He slid her an amused look. "What are you doing down here, Ashley?"

"I wanted to learn to fish. So I hired someone to teach me."

His brow rose. "Why this burning desire to fish?"

"I thought it was something you and I could do together. I wanted to surprise you."

He gave a short laugh and squeezed her hand. "Learning golf would have worked just as well and been a lot easier."

Ashley stopped beneath the shade of a maple tree and frowned up at him. "But I thought you enjoyed fishing."

He shrugged indifferently. "Sure, sometimes. But not in a little hole like Dale Hollow. The ocean is the only place to fish. That's where you catch the really big fish."

She remembered then that her father had asked her what kind of fishing she wanted to learn. She'd assumed Geoffrey enjoyed freshwater fishing. Obviously, she'd assumed wrong.

"Hey, it's okay, honey." Smiling, he tilted her chin up. "Don't worry about it. Your little escapade seems to have brought us a stroke of luck. If we work this right, we ought to be able to make a bit of money."

"Yeah," she agreed uneasily, wondering if she should tell him about the two hundred thousand dollars, then deciding to wait. "I guess we can."

He stepped closer. "Have I told you how much I love you?"

She shook her head, feeling a little stunned. He'd never said the words before. But she'd known he would—eventually. She'd been willing to wait for him to discover what she'd already decided for herself. Now he was telling her what she wanted to hear, and all she could do was stare at him stupidly.

"Well, I do. Last week I came to realize how much you mean to me. I really missed you, honey." He paused expectantly.

"I . . . I missed you, too." Even as she stumbled over the words she wasn't entirely certain she told the truth.

A sudden flash of anger shot through her. Damn Justin anyway. He had her so confused she couldn't think straight. Geoffrey was here, offering her what she knew she wanted, and she couldn't even respond properly.

Geoffrey smiled again. "I have something for you." Reaching into his pocket, he pulled out a small velvet-covered jeweler's box and handed it to her.

Ashley's hand trembled as she took the small gift. She stared down at it, rocked by the implications. It was too much, too fast. No, her mind fiercely denied. It was right. It was what she wanted and needed.

"I wanted to be a little more romantic about this, but I couldn't wait," Geoffrey said. "Go ahead and open it."

With her thumb, she pushed the lid upward. A perfectly cut diamond solitaire twinkled in the sunlight. "Oh, Geoffrey," she breathed, struck by the beauty of the ring. It was perfect, exactly what she might have picked for herself. More proof of how suited she and Geoffrey were for one another.

"I want you to be my wife, Ashley."

How like him to state what he wanted instead of asking in the traditional way. One of the things she liked most about him was his direct way of approaching things. There would be few surprises in their life together. But that's how she wanted it. Didn't she?

He took the ring out of its satiny bed and lifted her left hand to slip the ring onto her finger. It fit perfectly.

Ashley stared at the gorgeous diamond on her hand. Just a week ago she'd been anticipating this moment. Everything had worked out just as she'd planned. She should be thrilled. She had everything she wanted.

"Honey?"

She looked up into Geoffrey's confused eyes.

"Don't you like it?"

"It's beautiful," she assured him. "I'm just surprised, that's all."

"Pleasantly, I assume." He tipped his head to one side and smiled. "Do I at least get a kiss?"

"Of course." She stepped into his arms, lifting her hand to the back of his neck. With all her heart she wanted this kiss to stir something inside her. She wanted to feel it all the way to her toes. But she felt barely a flicker of heat when he drew away.

"Let's get out of here," he said, tugging on her hand. "We can get your things and head back to Knoxville tonight."

Ashley hung back. "I can't just leave, Geoffrey. I want to say goodbye to some people."

Irritation crept into his eyes. "Why? You don't really know any of these people. In a few days you'll forget all about them."

Unfortunately, she feared that was exactly what would happen. The thought saddened her more than she realized. She didn't want to forget about any of the people she'd met here on the Miles's farm.

"You go on to the car," she said. "I'll only be a few minutes."

"Okay." His agreement came reluctantly. "But don't be too long. I want to get home before dark."

"I'll hurry."

She turned and headed back toward the house. The football game had ended. People were milling about as usual, the air filled with voices and laughter. She was relieved to note that Justin wasn't part of the crowd. She didn't want to face him until she'd had a chance to tell Jessi and Cal goodbye.

She climbed the steps to the front porch, figuring she'd find Jessi inside, probably putting Angie down for a nap. Opening the screen door, she stepped into the living room and came face-to-face with Justin. She stopped, captured by the intensity of his gaze. His casual stance belied the tension radiating from him. As if it were a physical thing, she could feel it stealing from him, snaking around her, a very real danger.

"Is Jessi in here?" she asked, her voice barely above a whisper.

"She's cleaning up the kitchen floor. Angie dumped a glass of fruit juice."

"I just wanted to tell her goodbye." Forcing herself into motion, she moved to step around him.

His fingers clamped around her upper arm like a steel trap. Startled, she looked up into eyes glittering with turbulent emotions she didn't understand. She did recognize the fact that he wasn't going to make this easy for either of them.

She moistened her lips nervously. "I'm going back with Geoffrey."

"Are you?"

Beneath the silky tone she heard the unspoken challenge in his voice. She knew she needed to stay calm in order to survive this confrontation and walk away in one piece. "Please let go of my arm," she said evenly.

"Are you going to come clean and tell him about our night together?"

"We didn't . . . nothing really happened."

"Really."

His sardonic reply caused her to blush. Before she could form a response, he stepped closer, bringing with him his unique scent. Despite everything, Ashley felt her own senses respond. It took all her willpower not to reach for him or turn her head so that his lips could find hers.

His warm breath stirred the hair at her temple when he murmured, "A lot happened that night, Ashley. Denying it won't change the truth. I turned you inside out without even unzipping my pants."

She swallowed and closed her eyes. "Just let me go," she said, hating that she sounded so desperate.

"You're running, and we both know it. You don't love him, and we both know that."

How smug and knowledgeable he sounded. She felt a stab of fury and welcomed it. Her eyes opened and she jerked her arm. Still he held tight, infuriating her even more. "Don't you get it, Justin? It doesn't matter to me what you think. You don't matter to me. This week has just been a side trip in my life. In the whole scheme of things, it doesn't mean anything."

"So you've had your little fling and now you're going to return to your safe, boring existence." His fingers tightened, urging her closer. In a futile attempt to push him away, her hands came up to press against his chest. "Let's make sure you've gotten your money's worth," he said just before his mouth closed over hers.

Chapter Eight

Ashley stiffened, frightened by the powerful emotion gripping him and threatening to overtake her. Her mind insisted she fight. But in the end it was her own body that betrayed her when Justin's possession gentled. He loosened the grip on her arms and changed the slant of his mouth, deepening the kiss. Tenderly, his hands came up to frame her face.

Her senses responded instantly to his delicate caress. Even though she knew she was stumbling blind into a loaded minefield, she curled her fingers into his shirt front and leaned into his body. An overpowering rush of heat brought with it an unquenchable thirst for this one man. She couldn't come up with a reasonable explanation for it, and at this point she couldn't even think why it should matter. The control she clung to so tenaciously shattered into tiny fragments. Logic faded, as did the world around her. Her sole focus was Justin and the pleasure he gave her.

His hands skimmed down her back to her waist. Shifting slightly, he brought her closer still until their bodies were perfectly matched. She gripped his shoulders as he took his fill of her.

Passion flared, sending flames of desire dancing around and between and through them.

His mouth left hers to make a slow, moist trail toward her ear. She tipped her head to the side, relishing the delicious shivers skipping over her skin. His hands captured hers, his thumb brushed over the new diamond on her finger.

He tugged gently on her earlobe with his teeth before saying, "Shall I offer to educate your fiancé on what really turns you on, Ashley? I'd wager that I have more experience with you than he does."

His hurtful words registered in her hazy brain with exploding clarity. When he released her and stepped back, she stood alone, her body trembling with unfulfilled longing, her mind full of shame and remorse. Tears stung her eyes as she lifted her gaze to his. He stood with his arms folded across his chest, his feelings carefully hidden now by the bland expression on his face.

He appeared completely indifferent to the raging emotions battering her mentally and physically. Destroying her self-control was so easy for him. She despised him for exploiting her. She despised herself for being weak enough to allow him to do so.

"You must be very proud of yourself." She wrapped her arms around herself, trying to keep from shivering. "You brought me to my knees, Justin. You win."

He shook his head. "There are no winners here."

Pride demanded she walk away from him with her head held high. She drew in a deep breath, trying to ease the pressure in her chest. "I'll be the first to admit that there's a physical attraction between us. But what I feel for Geoffrey is stronger and deeper than anything you have to offer me. I'm sure he'll have no trouble exceeding your level of expertise."

A cold smile tilted up one side of his mouth. "You stand there with his ring on your finger, yet it was me you were responding to only seconds ago. I could have had you right here on Jessi's sofa and you wouldn't have made the slightest protest. How do you justify that, Ashley?"

He made it sound so ugly, made her sound so spineless.

"What do you want from me?" she demanded bitterly. "You keep chipping away at my plans, but what you're offering me isn't enough. This physical thing between us isn't enough for me, Justin."

"Why don't you take an uncalculated risk? Why don't you stay and see what's really at stake here?"

She stared at him. Could he really expect her to turn her whole life upside-down based on nothing more than her overactive libido? Dear God, she'd known him less than two weeks, and much of that time she'd spent in a state of confusion. How could he expect her to take a chance like that?

"I can't."

"Trust me."

His quiet request packed a punch she could never have prepared herself for. For a moment she allowed herself to consider what might happen if she trusted her heart to him. On many levels she did trust him. But it wasn't enough. He was asking more than she could give.

"I can't," she said again, silently begging him to understand. She watched as his eyes hardened and the mask of indifference returned to his features.

"You mean you won't. There's a big difference between can't and won't, Ashley. I can't make you stay. I can't make you pretty promises, and I can't give you iron-clad guarantees. You won't be honest with yourself, and you won't give what's between us a fair chance." He studied her a long moment, his emotions carefully concealed. "And I won't come after you if you leave this way." He shook his head. "I can't."

The truth hurt. The pain his words caused settled in her chest, threatening to suffocate her. Raw emotion clawed at her from all sides, and she knew there wasn't anything left to be said. To continue this battle would only guarantee her embarrassing defeat.

She turned and walked to the door. Stopping there, she looked at him over her shoulder. "Would you please tell Jessi and Cal thanks, and that I'll be in touch with Jessi about the figurines?"

He didn't move a muscle. "Sure."

The ticking of the clock marked the passage of time as their gazes locked and held. His expression didn't reveal even a flicker of regret.

Something moved through her. For some reason she needed for him to understand. "Justin—"

"Just go."

The two words had the impact of a physical blow. Turning away, she darted out the door. With her head bent, she hurried to Geoffrey's car, hoping every step of the way he wouldn't notice how upset she was.

As Geoffrey pulled out onto the road, Ashley couldn't keep from looking back one last time at the sprawling farmhouse. She saw Justin standing on the porch, watching her go. His image blurred behind a wall of tears before disappearing completely.

Justin continued to stare at the point where Anderson's car had disappeared around a bend in the road. People milled around him, yet he felt completely alone. All that registered in his mind was that Ashley was gone, and that he'd sent her away with ugly words and accusations. He didn't understand why he'd done it. He thought he'd reconciled in his mind that she wouldn't be staying. But something snapped when he'd seen her in Anderson's arms. He'd wanted to hurt her, and he'd succeeded. Vaguely, he wondered if his absolute lack of emotion at the moment was normal under the circumstances.

He felt an arm slip around his waist and looked over as Jessi joined him. She gave him a guarded smile.

"I suppose you heard most of that classy exchange?" he asked ruefully.

"A little. I'm sorry, Justin."

"For what? Being in your own house?"

"No. I'm sorry you're hurting."

He wanted to deny it, but knew he'd be lying. He suspected that when this numbness wore off, he'd hurt a lot more. For Jessi he managed a tight smile. "I've hurt before. I'll survive."

Jessi stepped away from him and leaned a hip against

the railing. "If it helps any, you've got a lot of friends around here."

"I know."

"Hey," Cal said as he climbed the steps to the porch. "Did I see Ashley leave with that Anderson guy?"

Justin nodded. "She said to tell you two thanks."

Cal frowned as he slipped an arm around Jessi's shoulders. "She just up and left with the guy?"

"Looks that way." In an effort to sidetrack Cal from asking more questions, Justin looked at Jessi and said, "She also said she'd be in touch with you about the figurines."

"She offered to let me set up a display of the Family Folks in her shop." Jessi couldn't keep her excitement from showing as she looked from Justin to her husband.

"That's great," Justin said, sharing in her happiness.

"Yeah, I'm pretty excited."

"This could open some doors for you, honey," Cal said. "Who knows? Maybe your Family Folks will make us rich!"

Jessi laughed as he hugged her close.

Justin watched the happy couple and felt the first sting of regret stir his soul. Yeah, he'd hurt before, and he'd survived. But this time surviving seemed like little more than a waste of time.

Ashley wasn't sure at what point she'd lost all control of her life. Perhaps it had been the moment the giant smallmouth had latched onto her lure and she'd set the hook. Deep in her heart she suspected it had been the moment she'd turned her back on Justin and shut him out of her life.

Only three weeks had passed since she'd left Windsong and returned to Knoxville with Geoffrey. She had no idea so much could change in such a short period of time. She barely recognized her life or herself these days.

In her office, she settled back in the high back leather chair and viewed the scattered paperwork on her desk. She had nearly two hours before the shop opened for business, and intended to at least make a dent in the mess before her.

She began by sorting everything into three stacks: bills, correspondence, and filing. Paying the bills was top priority and answering the letters was next. The filing could wait. Pushing everything else out of her mind, she began to organize the chaos. In this one area of her life she was determined to gain some control.

When the antique grandfather clock in the front hall struck nine o'clock, Ashley was amazed at how fast the time had passed. She'd at least conquered the bills. If anyone called, she could honestly say the check was in the mail.

Rising, she removed the cash drawer from the safe and carried it out to the register in front. After being certain everything was in order, she walked to the door and unlocked it. Collectibles and More was officially open for business.

Nancy York, one of the part-time workers, came in at nine-thirty to help with the morning routine. There were several browsers and a few sales made. All in all, it was a typical morning.

Just after noon the door opened and Ashley glanced up from the inventory list she was reviewing. Immediately, she tensed, recognizing the man who'd just entered her shop. She couldn't remember which of the sensational tabloid papers Vic Myers worked for, but she remembered distinctly that she hadn't liked him when he'd interviewed her the first time. His whole demeanor reminded her of a snake—sneaky and dangerous. Willing herself to relax, she waited while he slowly made his way across the room.

"Miss Harper." He reached his hand across the glass counter to her.

"Mr. Myers." She accepted the brief handshake, but afterward had to stop herself from wiping her hand down her skirt. Something about the man made her skin crawl.

"You remember my name," he said with a self-satisfied smirk. "Considering all the people you've talked to, that's pretty impressive."

"What brings you back?" she asked bluntly. "I'm busy right now."

"All I need is a few minutes of your time."

She stepped out from behind the counter and gestured toward the back. "Ten minutes."

Once inside her office, she saw him make a visual sweep of the room before turning his attention to her. "How can I help you, Mr. Myers?"

"Well, it's been nearly a month since you caused such a stir by catching that giant smallmouth bass at Dale Hollow. I just thought I'd check to see how things are going for you."

She shrugged as she moved around to stand behind her desk. "Things are going fine."

He reached inside his rumpled tan sports jacket and pulled out a voice-activated tape recorder. "Do you mind if I record our conversation?"

"No." She hated it, but she wasn't about to let him know. She'd keep control here if it killed her.

"Thanks." He set the tiny machine in the center of her desk. "How has your life changed since you returned from your fishing trip?"

"Other than being bombarded by the media, it hasn't," she lied. "I've had some offers to endorse some products, which I haven't decided on yet. If the press would leave me alone, I'd hardly notice any difference at all."

"Give us a break, Miss Harper," he cajoled. "Everybody loves a rags-to-riches story."

"I was hardly in rags to begin with. Besides, isn't it getting to be old news by now?"

"People are still talking about it. Don't you go to New York in a couple of weeks to collect your two hundred thousand dollars from Still Waters?"

Despite her surprise at his question, Ashley managed to keep her composure. "Nothing has been finalized," she answered smoothly, wondering how he'd found out about her plans.

"Well, when you do go to New York, whenever that may be, and you do collect your money, are you planning to split it with Justin Holmes?"

Ashley felt her pulse scramble and mentally berated herself. She had to get over this foolish habit she had of reacting every time she heard Justin's name. "Mr. Holmes has declined to accept any of the money."

The reporter nodded. "That's what he told me, too. I talked to him recently." He frowned at her. "Why do you suppose he declined?"

Ashley felt her nerves tighten. She didn't like this man or his questions. "You should have asked Mr. Holmes that question."

"I did. He told me it was none of my business."

She nearly smiled, imagining Justin's delivery of that message. "I think I would have to agree with him, Mr. Myers."

"You know, I have a theory about why Justin Holmes doesn't want any of your money."

"I'm not interested in your theories." She glanced at her watch. "And your ten minutes are up."

"I'll be quick," he promised. "I think your two-hundred grand must seem pretty meager to a man who's already a millionaire and set to inherit a multi-million dollar family empire." His eyes narrowed slightly as he watched her. "You did know about his connection with Holmes Enterprises, didn't you, Miss Harper?"

"I hired Mr. Holmes to teach me to fish and that's exactly what he did." She shrugged. "Besides, when did it become a crime in this country to be heir to a legitimate family business? I think you're trying to make a story where there is none, Mr. Myers."

"You've got to admit it makes for an interesting story line."

She reached out and depressed the stop button on his recorder. "If you'll excuse me, Mr. Myers, I've got a business to run."

He picked up the recorder and put it in his pocket. "Have a nice day, Miss Harper. I'll show myself out."

Once he was gone, she reached up to rub her forehead. Tension throbbed there, dull and persistent.

It wasn't the catch of the record smallmouth bass that stirred people's interest now. It was the money that had complete strangers writing her letters and leaving messages on her answering machine. She didn't know how to deal with the pleas for financial help, and she didn't trust the unsolicited advice offered to her about investing the money. Even Geoffrey's ideas about the money were too far-fetched or risky for her peace of mind.

With a weary sigh she began to pace the office. At one point she'd thought she could handle all the hype. But she'd been in Windsong then, and Justin had been there to help her. She remembered how easily he'd handled the media the day the mayor had called the press conference. Justin had fielded the majority of questions, shielding her from the glare of publicity. He'd been more than willing to help her. What she wouldn't give for his steady assistance now.

She could call him.

Immediately, she rejected the idea, thinking of their last encounter. She wished now she could erase the ugly words they'd exchanged. She wished she'd never left the way she had. But Geoffrey's arrival had caught her off guard, and she hadn't been thinking clearly about anything. Actually, she couldn't remember what her last clear thought had been.

A light knock on the door interrupted her circling thoughts. She turned as a worried-looking Nancy stepped into the office.

"We've got a problem out front," Nancy said, her voice pitched low. "Mrs. Stratton is here insisting that she ordered two vases three weeks ago and that you assured her they'd be in by today."

Ashley nodded. "I took the order myself. The vases aren't here?"

"No, and I can't find any record that they were ordered. The computer shows nothing for Mrs. Stratton."

Ashley felt a tremor of panic. She remembered taking the order over the phone. That day, that whole week, had been a nightmare. The press had come and gone at will, and the phone had rung incessantly. And in the middle of all that, Liz Stratton had called and placed an order for two crystal and gold limited series vases.

"Oh, no," Ashley whispered. "Did I forget to place the order?"

"It looks like you did. What are we going to do?"

Ashley drew a deep, calming breath. "I'll take care of it." She headed for the door, mentally preparing herself to deal with a very wealthy, very demanding, and about to be very upset Liz Stratton.

"I still don't see what you're so upset about," Geoffrey said as he mixed a drink and carried it out to the balcony where Ashley sat at the small patio table. "Liz Stratton is a first-class bitch and everyone knows it. Why didn't you just let her walk out?"

"Because it was my mistake and she's a good customer. I owed it to her to at least try to make it right."

For the past half hour Ashley had been trying to make Geoffrey understand why she'd sold Mrs. Stratton the vases at below cost. Looking at his face now she could see that he still didn't follow her logic. It occurred to her that she and Geoffrey hadn't been agreeing on much of anything lately.

With a shrug, he sat down across from her. "You're losing money on the deal."

"But hopefully I'm not losing her business, and whoever else's she might influence."

"What difference is it going to make? In a couple of weeks you won't even need to go into the shop. Why don't you sell it and save yourself the headache of dealing with all those demanding people."

Ashley frowned at him. She'd endured an awful day, her head still pounded and the bit of sympathy and support she'd hoped for from her fiancé was not forthcoming. Now, out of the blue, he was suggesting she give up her business.

"What are you talking about?" she asked. "Why would I want to sell the shop?"

"Why keep it? After you collect the money from Still Waters you won't need to work anymore. Why tie yourself down to something that causes more headaches than it's worth?"

Her brow arched in shocked wonder. "Exactly what do you expect me to do with my time?"

"We can travel."

"Travel?" Ashley felt her temper begin to sizzle. What she didn't need after a day like today was Geoffrey totally rearranging her life without her knowledge. "Did you have a destination in mind?"

He leaned forward, his eyes bright with anticipation. "Anywhere we want, honey. We can see the world."

"What about your job?"

"What about it? I can quit at any time." He grinned and reached for her hand. "You know, I've just had a fantastic idea. Let's get married while we're in New York."

Her irritation increased. Lately, Geoffrey was full of great ideas and extravagant plans. He was rapidly spending money she didn't even possess.

"I want to get married here in church, you know that," she reminded him stiffly.

"But just think of it. We could get married in New York and then fly to Paris for our honeymoon. How much more romance could a woman want?"

Ashley pulled her hand free and stood. "No, Geoffrey. I don't want to go to Paris."

"It's *your* money so we have to do everything *your* way. Is that how it works, Ashley?" He stood and slammed his chair against the table.

Startled by his unexpected outburst, she stared at him, unable to form a reply.

"I never realized how inflexible you are," he continued. "You don't know how to relax and have a good time. You have to plan everything out to the last little detail."

"That's not true! I can have as much fun as the next person."

"Name the last time!"

In Windsong. She almost blurted out the truth before stopping herself. "Look, Geoffrey," she said wearily. "Two hundred thousand dollars isn't enough money for us to retire and live like the idle rich. Besides, after I pay taxes, there won't even be that much. If we invest it wisely, we'll be able to live comfortably and still have a good time."

"My God, do you hear yourself? Have you ever in your entire life had an impractical thought or a spontaneous moment?"

A vision of Justin carrying her into his bedroom exploded inside Ashley's mind. She'd been spontaneous that night. In fact, she'd been willing to throw all caution aside and be irresponsibly spontaneous. Justin had been the practical one, sacrificing his own needs for her protection.

"I can't live a rigid life, Ashley. You're going to have to loosen up a lot or our marriage will never work."

She looked at him, really looked, seeing past what she perceived him to be to the real person. She didn't like what she saw.

"I didn't realize you were such a free spirit," she said dully.

He shrugged. "Life gets pretty boring if you don't shake it up every now and then." He hesitated. "Maybe we . . . I don't know. Maybe we should rethink getting married. Maybe we don't know each other as well as we thought."

She nearly laughed at the irony of the moment. Instead, she said simply, "I think you're probably right."

He took a step back, looking uncomfortable. "I . . . we'll talk tomorrow."

She nodded. "Good night, Geoffrey."

Without further comment, she followed him inside and watched as he left the apartment. Once the door closed behind him, she looked down at his ring. The diamond had lost all its sparkle.

Ashley loved her father's den. Within the warmth of walnut-panelled walls and shelves of law books, she'd spent the best part of her growing-up years. It hadn't struck her as odd that she'd felt the need to come here tonight.

After her heart-to-heart with Geoffrey, she'd taken two aspirin for her headache and a hot shower for the tension eating at her. Sleep had eluded her until finally, she'd dressed in old jeans and a tee shirt and climbed into her car to take a drive. Thirty minutes later, she pulled into her father's driveway. It was eleven-thirty when she rang the doorbell.

He escorted her into his den and turned off the late-night television he'd been watching. They settled into the old leather sofa, just like they used to, and he listened as she launched into a recital of the day she'd had, minus the argument with Geoffrey.

Tucking her legs up beneath her, she leaned her head back and sighed. "All this business with the fish is making me crazy, Dad. I can't seem to get things under control."

"I thought Geoffrey was helping you."

"He's mainly interested in the offers that are going to make us some money. Those are the ones he's taking care of. But my biggest problem is the media. It's leaked out now that I'll be going to New York soon. And a reporter for one of the tabloids has made the connection between Justin and his father."

"Oh, boy. That's going to make some headlines."

"No kidding." She paused before saying, "Why didn't you tell me about Justin?"

Nick frowned. "What should I have told you?"

"That you had a big impact on his life. You taught him to fish, didn't you?"

Nick smiled and nodded. "Justin and I crossed paths at a time when we both needed someone to listen and to care. I was missing your mother and overwhelmed with the responsibility of raising two young girls. Justin, on the other hand, was rebelling against a life-style he knew he didn't want, but was destined to inherit. On some basic level we were able to connect and help each other through a rough patch. It was as simple as that. When you told me you wanted someone to teach you to fish, I thought of him." He studied her a moment. "Did I make a mistake?"

She shook her head. "I don't know. He turned my world upside-down before I even caught the fish."

"Well, Justin tends to have a way of turning things upside-down. His father can attest to that."

"Is it bad between them? He wouldn't talk much about it."

Nick sighed. "Well, J.T. was furious when Justin walked

out, but I don't think he was really shocked. Justin knew
from an early age that he wasn't cut out for the corporate
world. What frustrated J.T. most was that Justin was a natural to take over Holmes Enterprises. He's very intelligent
and possesses a keen business sense. J.T. could have rested
easy turning the reins over to him.''

"Has J.T. seen Justin since he left?"

"I don't think so. I think they're both stubborn and
neither one will make the first move." Nick shrugged.
"The funny thing is, I know J.T. respects Justin for the
stand he took. Once he recovered from the shock, he
couldn't fault his son for his actions. After all, J.T. always
preached that it was important to be your own man. Justin
was doing just that.''

"They why don't they see one another and mend the
relationship?"

"It's probably easier now to let the rift stand. Mending
relationships can be very painful."

Ashley looked away from her father. She thought about
mending her relationship with Justin. Would he let her
back into his life and give her another chance? Is that what
she really wanted? Could she trust in him, love him, the
way he needed?

"I'm not going to marry Geoffrey," she confessed.

Nick reached out and brushed a hand down her hair.
"I can't say I'm sorry, sweetheart."

"I know you don't like him."

"I just don't think he's the right man for you, Ashley."

She looked over at him. "Do you know I've never
believed in romantic love?"

He frowned. "I don't think I understand."

"All those romantic things you hear about in love songs,
I've never believed in those things. I've never thought that
they actually existed."

"Why?"

"Because I've never seen any living proof of them. As a
matter of fact, the main reason I wanted to marry Geoffrey
was because I was sure it was more important to have a
compatible relationship based on the things you have in

common with someone, rather than on some fleeting emotion."

"But love, if it's real, isn't a fleeting emotion, Ashley."

"But I never understood that. Justin told me that after being with you that summer he decided he never wanted to love anyone as much as you loved mom. He said he never wanted to risk that kind of pain. Then he said that once he grew up, he realized how special the love you and mom shared was. He said it would be worth the pain."

Nick's hand came down to cup her chin. "Ashley, I'm so sorry I didn't do a better job of letting you know how much your mother meant to me." He hesitated, searching her eyes. "She was everything wonderful in my life. My most fervent wish is that you and Sara find loves just as wonderful."

She felt tears burning her eyes and blinked against them. "What does that kind of love feel like, Daddy?" she whispered.

He reached for her hand and linked their fingers. "It's a feeling that fills your heart and claims your mind," he answered, his voice husky. "You just know this one person is the only one you'll need in this lifetime. It's not a logical conclusion. It's a heart-felt conclusion. It's frightening and thrilling and worth every risk you have to take."

Tears traced down Ashley cheeks as Nick reached to pull her close. He cradled her head on his shoulder just as he'd done all those years ago. "Don't settle for anything less, Ashley. Wait for the real thing."

What she couldn't tell him just then was that when she left Windsong, she may have walked away from her one chance for the real thing.

Chapter Nine

Ashley spent a restless night at her father's house. By the time the sun rose the next morning she'd come to a few concrete decisions regarding her life.

She enjoyed a leisurely breakfast with Nick, before driving home to shower and change. It was nearly ten when she arrived at the shop. As she entered through the back and went into her office, she could hear Sara talking with a customer.

After stowing her purse in the bottom drawer of her desk, Ashley sat down and reached for the phone. Her first call was to Geoffrey. He didn't answer, but she left a message on his answering machine asking him to meet her later in the day at her apartment. She intended to officially break the engagement then.

Next, she called Jessi Miles. It was a short conversation since Jessi was on her way out the door. Ashley quickly made arrangements for Jessi to bring her collection of Family Folks to the shop on Friday.

After Ashley hung up the phone she wished she'd had to nerve to ask about Justin.

"Good morning." Sara appeared in the doorway.

The two sisters barely resembled one another. Ashley

was tall and willowy, Sara, petite and curvy. Her eyes were darker than Ashley's and her hair shorter and lighter. The physical differences were dramatic, but the emotional bond between the two women was very strong. In many ways Sara had been Ashley's surrogate mother.

Ashley smiled. "Hi. Things busy this morning?"

"The usual. I did sell one of the collector's plates." A frown creased her forehead. "Why did you come in? You look really wiped out this morning."

"Restless night. I had a lot of things to sort out."

"Well, that's all fine and good, but if you don't start getting some rest, you're going to drop in your tracks."

"Yes, mother," Ashley teased.

"I'm serious," Sara replied, looking just that. "You haven't been yourself since you came back from your trip."

"Well, catching that fish did kind of shake up my life."

"No." Sara shook her head and stepped into the office. "It's not the fish. I thought it was, and I know that's what you want everyone to believe, but that's not it." She reached for a framed photograph on the corner of Ashley's desk. The picture had only been there a couple of days. Ashley couldn't even explain why she'd put it there. It was a shot of her and Justin with the fish. They'd been laughing when the moment had been captured on film, and she liked the feeling she got when she looked at it.

"I think," Sara said thoughtfully, "that what happened to you is about six-feet tall and handsome as sin." She looked at Ashley and arched a brow. "I think my baby sister has fallen in love for real."

Ashley began to shuffle through a stack of papers on her desk. "Come on, Sara. Let's don't get started on this."

"You can't marry Geoffrey if you're in love with another man. Marrying Geoffrey is a big mistake anyway, but now you . . ." Her voice trailed off and she abruptly reached across the desk to catch Ashley's left wrist. "You're not wearing his ring."

The two sisters regarded one another a long, silent moment. Finally, Ashley sighed and withdrew her hand. "I'm breaking the engagement," she said as she leaned back in her chair.

Sara placed a hand over her heart and closed her eyes. "Thank you, God," she whispered with heartfelt gratitude.

"Oh, stop it." It was humbling to discover everyone thought her engagement to Geoffrey was a big mistake when she'd been so sure of herself.

"He's just not right for you," Sara said simply. She tapped a fingertip against the frame. "This is the guy for you."

"Well, I hate to disappoint you, but that guy doesn't like me much."

Sara peered at the photograph closely. Smiling smugly, she set it back on Ashley's desk. "That man is crazy in love with you."

Ashley felt tears sting her eyes. She wanted more than anything to believe her sister's words. But then she remembered the way Justin had looked when they'd parted. He hadn't loved her then. He'd despised her.

"Call him," Sara urged softly. "Or better yet, go back to him. Whatever went wrong can be fixed."

Ashley shook her head. "It was a very ugly scene. I'm afraid it may be beyond fixing."

"But you won't know until you try, will you? And you can't go on like this. It's eating you alive, Ashley. You have to go back and talk to him."

"I'm afraid."

Sara blinked once, then gave a short laugh. "Afraid? You? Good grief, you jump out of airplanes. How can you be afraid of one man?"

"I've been afraid of Justin since the day I met him."

"You're afraid of yourself," Sara stated bluntly, unknowingly echoing Justin's words. "Or, more likely, you're afraid of what you feel for this guy because you can't box it into some neat little category."

The bells at the front door sounded, indicating that someone had entered the shop.

"Go back and settle things one way or another," Sara advised sternly before turning away and leaving the room.

Ashley took a moment to close her eyes. The headache was back, or still with her. She wasn't sure which. Sara made everything sound so simple. All Ashley had to do was return to Windsong and talk to Justin. But all she could remember was the cold disdain in Justin's eyes as she'd turned and walked away from him.

She opened her eyes, her gaze drifting to the photograph. Leaning forward, she picked it up and studied it closely. She'd been happy when the shutter had clicked and captured the moment. Truly happy. And it had nothing to do with the fish or the money. It was the man. She'd been in love even then and too stubborn to admit it. No, she decided, she hadn't been stubborn. She'd been terrified. It had been easy to plan a life with Geoffrey. She'd had so little to lose. Planning a life with Justin was a completely different matter. She'd have to lay it all on the line, knowing he'd take nothing less than all she had. But she also knew he'd demand no more than he was willing to give back to her.

She touched her fingertips to his image. He'd been happy that day, too. She wondered if she'd destroyed that happiness for both of them. She wondered if she had the courage to go back and find out.

Justin had known it would only be a matter of time. Judging by the way his morning was going, he knew the connection between himself and Holmes Enterprises had become common knowledge. He'd suspected it when he'd stepped into the bank and had been personally greeted by Sam Carson, the bank president. That had never happened before.

But he'd been positive when he'd gone into Peabody's Grocery. Bea Jenkins had addressed him with a very formal "Good morning, Mr. Holmes" instead of her usual, "Morning, Justin. How are the fish biting?" The feisty cashier was old enough to be his grandmother and had a penchant for slightly ribald jokes. She never failed to have a new one to share with him. Except today. Today she'd wished him a good day and sent him on his way.

Justin could feel the muscle tick in his jaw as he carried his two bags of groceries toward the Blazer. He knew if he didn't release the pressure of his clenched teeth soon, he'd have a permanently locked jaw.

Damn it all anyway. He figured he had that slimy reporter Vic Myers to thank for this. Everyone else he'd talked to had been interested in the fish or Ashley or the part Justin had played in the whole scenario. Everyone except Vic Myers. He'd been more interested in why Justin had declined to split the money with Ashley. Justin had suspected his days of anonymity were numbered. Apparently he'd been right.

He stowed the groceries in the back of his truck and slipped his hand into his pocket to retrieve his keys. He'd just unlocked the driver's door when a car pulled into the parking spot beside him. He glanced up and saw it was Jessi and Angie. Within seconds the little girl was out of the car and racing toward him.

"Hi, Justin!"

He scooped her up and hugged her close. At least there was one person in Windsong who wasn't intimidated by his identity.

Angie drew back and lifted her pudgy hands to his face. "Where you been, Justin?" she asked, her little face creased with a frown.

He knew what she was asking. He hadn't been out for a Sunday get-together since Ashley left. "I've been really busy," he said. "Have you missed me?" He grinned as she nodded vigorously.

"Hi, Justin." Jessi came to stand beside them.

Justin looked at her, wondering if he'd really heard a note of reticence in her voice or if he'd just imagined it. "How is everybody?"

"We're all fine." She reached up to take Angie from him. "Let me take her. She had a sucker from the bank and I'm sure she's covered in it. She'll get it all over you."

He drew back slightly. "She's fine," he said quietly. "I've never been bothered by sticky fingers."

An uncomfortable silence stretched between them as he held her gaze. He nearly choked on his frustration. He'd thought Jessi was the least likely person to be affected by the news about him. Looking at her now, he realized he'd thought wrong.

He shifted Angie in his arms. "Do I look different to you, Jessi?"

Her brow arched in surprise. "No, of course not."

"Then don't treat me any differently. Nothing's changed."

"I'm sorry," she said softly. "You're right. I just don't know many millionaires, Justin. It's a little unsettling."

He nearly swore, then remembered he still held Angie. She grinned at him and patted his cheek. He looked back at Jessi. "You got time to talk?"

She smiled and visibly relaxed. "Sure."

When he suggested they walk to the park, Angie squealed and clapped her hands. Justin settled her onto his shoulders as they walked the half-block to the city park. The playground equipment was deserted, giving Angie her choice of rides. She directed him toward the swings.

Jessi stood to the side as Justin pushed Angie's swing. Little girl laughter echoed in the early morning air.

He shot Jessi a quick look. "How did you find out?"

"Aunt Lila called me yesterday. She heard it from Sandy Hall at the Marina. I guess some reporter was in town a few days ago asking a lot of questions about you."

Justin grimaced. "I guess I can assume the whole town knows?"

"I think it would be a good bet." Jessi shrugged. "News like that makes the rounds in a hurry, Justin. Especially in a town like Windsong. You should know that."

He nodded and turned his attention back to Angie, making certain not to push her too high.

"Was your life so bad?" Jessi asked. "Is that why you left it all behind?"

"No. Relatively speaking it was a great life. It just wasn't mine."

"Meaning what exactly?"

"Meaning it's difficult living in the shadow of a man like J.T. Holmes. I never wanted for anything, Jessi. But the flip side of that is that I never knew who I really was or what I was really capable of. Everything filtered through

J.T. It wasn't until I came here that I knew what it was to stand on my own. What I've accomplished here had nothing to do with my father or Holmes Enterprises. It's strictly mine."

"Squirrels!" Angie shouted as she started to wriggle in the swing. Justin caught her around the waist and lifted her from the plastic seat before she managed to fall. He set her on her feet and smiled as she instantly charged off after three squirrels under a huge oak tree. He and Jessi followed at a more leisurely pace.

"Did you leave on bad terms?" Jessi asked.

"With my father. We haven't spoken for eight years. I still see my mother and my brother and sister."

"So your father was angry? He didn't want you to leave?"

Justin gave a rueful laugh. "He was furious, which was nothing less than I expected."

They stopped and watched as Angie ran in circles trying to capture her prey. Finally all three squirrels scurried up the tree, leaving her at the bottom to stare up at them helplessly.

She turned to Justin and pointed upward. "Lift me up!"

He chuckled and picked her up. "I think you're out of luck, kiddo. Those little guys are just too quick for you." At her look of disappointment, he gave her a kiss and enjoyed her carefree laughter. "We better get back to the store so your mom can get her shopping done."

As they made their way back to the grocery, Jessi looked over at him. "Do you regret leaving as you did, Justin?"

He shook his head. "Not the leaving. I regret that the rift between J.T. and myself hasn't been resolved."

"Why don't you just call him or go see him?"

Justin thought about the last time he and his father had spoken. Hurtful things had been said on both sides. He and J.T. had both burned their bridges pretty thoroughly. "Some things aren't easily mended."

"I don't believe that. You know how I feel about family. As far as I'm concerned, there's nothing more important."

They stopped beside his Blazer. "I know how you feel," he said, meeting her gaze. "It's made clear every Sunday I spend with you and your family."

"We've missed you. Everyone's come to think of you as family."

"Well, that's probably changed now."

"It shouldn't. You don't look any different to me."

He grinned. "Thanks."

"Give folks a little time," she advised. "They may feel a little awkward right now, but it'll pass."

He nodded, hoping she was right. Maybe if he just went on as if nothing had changed, everyone else would too. Maybe.

Angie began to kick her legs restlessly. "I want down."

Justin bent and set her on the ground. "See you later, sweetie."

She leaned over and kissed his cheek. "Bye, Justin."

As he straightened, Jessi reached for the little girl's hand. "By the way, I'm going to Knoxville on Friday to see Ashley about displaying my Family Folks in her shop."

The unexpected mention of Ashley's name jolted him. He'd done his level best to forget about her. And he'd failed miserably.

"Good luck," he said simply. "I hope it works out for you."

"Thank you. Would you like to send a message to Ashley?"

"No. I think it's all been said."

Jessi's eyes narrowed as she regard him. "You know, Justin, you've already got one rift in your life that you regret. Do you really think you can handle two?"

He drew in a deep breath. "I appreciate what you're trying to do, Jess—"

"But mind my own business," she finished for him.

He smiled wryly. "Something like that."

She shrugged. "I had to try."

"I know." He reached into his pocket and pulled out his keys. "Have a safe trip. I'll talk to you when you get back."

"Thanks. Take care, Justin."

He watched as she and Angie turned and headed for the grocery. The dull, vacant ache in his chest that had become a permanent part of his existence lately, intensified. All it took was the mention of Ashley's name. He wondered when it would get easier, if it ever would. It did no good to remind himself that Ashley had made her choice, that she'd made it clear she wanted nothing he had to offer. The sooner he accepted that fact, the better off he'd be. Unfortunately, his heart wasn't nearly as pragmatic as his brain. And it was his heart that refused to believe that Ashley was gone for good. His foolish heart still harbored a tiny seed of hope that Ashley would return to him.

"So where did you leave Angie today?" Ashley looked across the linen-covered table to Jessi.

"Cal's mother is looking after her." Jessi smiled. "As a matter of fact, she's keeping her for the weekend. Cal's coming to meet me tonight. It's been a long time since we've had a chance to get away by ourselves."

Ashley studied the other woman, noting the slight flush on her cheeks. After all the years of marriage, Jessi was still excited about spending time with her husband. Ashley felt an uncomfortable stab of envy, followed quickly by guilt. She really didn't begrudge Jessi her happiness. She just didn't quite understand it.

"Sounds like fun," she said. "Do you have anything special planned?"

Jessi shook her head. "Not really. The change of scenery will be good for both of us, I think. We'll just relax and see some of the sights around here."

"Sounds like fun." Ashley took a drink of her water. She might as well ask now and get it out of the way. Trying to sound casual, she said, "How's Justin?"

"Busy. His business has picked up since you caught that fish."

"That's good."

"He's not very happy about his background leaking out, but he's handling it."

"Does the whole town know?"

"Oh, sure. It's been at the top of the gossip list for a few days now. I saw Justin in town a couple of days ago. I actually felt a little awkward when I saw him. He set me straight pretty quickly."

"I'll bet he did."

"He hasn't been out for a Sunday get-together since you left."

Ashley intentionally ignored the subtle implication of that statement and said, "Well, if he's been busy, he probably just hasn't had time."

"Probably. I just hope he doesn't decide to leave Windsong."

Ashley frowned. "Is he thinking about it?"

"Not that I know of, but after all that's happened, I wouldn't be surprised if he did." She looked up as the waiter approached with their lunch.

Ashley thought about Jessi's observation as their food was served. If Justin left Windsong, where would he go? Back to New York? What if he left and she wasn't able to find him? Was she willing to chance that happening?

"This looks wonderful," Jessi said after the waiter departed, drawing Ashley's attention away from her troubled thoughts. "Thank you for lunch. And for giving me a place to display my Family Folks."

"That makes thank you number seventeen, I think," Ashley chided as she cut into her boneless chicken.

"I can't help it, Ashley. It's a really nice thing you're doing."

"You've got talent. Is that something else that runs in your family like the great cooks?"

Jessi nodded. "Everyone seems to do some kind of craft. Aunt Rose and Aunt Myra both quilt. A few of the others do different kinds of needlework. Several work with me on the ceramics. I really think between all of us we could pretty well stock our own shop. Do you think a shop like yours would work in Windsong?"

Ashley chewed thoughtfully before shaking her had. "I don't think so. My shop is geared more toward expensive collectibles. I don't think we could get the clientele I have now to drive all the way to Windsong to buy what they can find right here in Knoxville."

"You're probably right."

Ashley took a drink of her iced tea before saying, "I do think a shop in Windsong featuring local handcrafted items could be very successful. People interested in that sort of product seem to have no misgivings about driving out of their way to acquire that special something they're searching for. It's as if the drive adds to the appeal. I think a shop in Windsong is a great idea."

"And expensive. I've checked into leasing some space in town." Jessi shook her head. "I just can't afford to do it."

"Maybe a place out closer to the highway would be a better location."

"There's nothing out there."

"What if we bought some land and built something?"

Jessi frowned and stared across the table. "We?"

Smiling, Ashley nodded. "Jessi, I need to invest part of my money from catching Beauregard into something. How do you feel about being business partners?"

"Are you kidding?" Jessi's eyes grew as wide as saucers. "Ashley, I'm beginning to think you must be my fairy godmother."

Justin decided he was just about as tired as he'd ever been in his entire thirty-five years. He'd stumbled into the cabin a little before six that morning after an all-night fishing session. He'd managed to shed his boots, socks, and shirt before collapsing onto the sofa. His last coherent thought had been that he was getting too damned old for back-to-back all-nighters.

Sometime later he opened bleary eyes and tried to focus on the clock across the room. He thought it read eleven-fifteen but wouldn't swear to it. Sitting up, he ran his hands over his face in an effort to chase away the clinging remnants of sleep. A two-days growth of beard scratched against his palms. Definitely a shower and shave were in order. And then a hot meal. Maybe at that point he'd start to feel human again.

He pushed to his feet and paused, the sound of an approaching vehicle catching his attention. He swore softly, sure another pesky reporter was about to turn up on his doorstep. If one more person asked for an interview ... Swearing again, he rubbed a hand over face. He'd declined all requests, including the one Denny Whiteside had practically demanded of him.

Unfortunately, Justin's silence hadn't kept him from being the feature story in magazines and newspapers across the country. He hadn't bothered to read any of them, because he really didn't give a damn what was being written about him. He knew, however, that they had to be filled with speculations and old information.

His mother had called earlier in the week to inform him that the reporters were busy on that end, too, and that J.T. wasn't happy with the unexpected scrutiny. At least that was one point Justin and his father agreed on.

On top of all the nonsense, Still Waters was hosting an extravagant public relations event next week in order to award Ashley her money. They'd asked Justin to attend. He honestly didn't now if they wanted him there because he'd been Ashley's fishing guide, or because it would be a publicity coup for them to be the first to lure Holmes Enterprises' elusive heir out into the open.

God, he was sick of the whole affair. He just wanted to go to sleep and wake up to find his life as calm and peaceful as it had been before Ashley Harper had stepped into it.

He listened as the vehicle drew nearer. He definitely wasn't in the mood to talk to anyone today. Dudley had been good about announcing the arrival of strangers. Most of them had been unwilling to venture out of their cars with the dog barking loudly from the porch. Justin didn't believe for a minute the pooch would actually take a bite out of anyone, but he looked pretty convincing just the same. So he'd just let Dudley do his thing this morning and wait for his unwanted visitor to leave.

As Justin stood there listening, the dog began to bark as expected. As usual, he sounded vicious enough. But over the racket of the dog on the porch, Justin heard the sound of a car door slamming. Obviously, his uninvited guest wasn't about to be deterred by a barking dog.

Abruptly, Dudley quieted, and through the open windows Justin could hear the soft murmur of a woman's voice. Response stirred deep inside, even as his mind told him he was imagining impossible things. But when he walked to the door and pushed it open, there was no denying the truth before him.

She stood there dressed in a denim jumper and a bright pink tee shirt. Her fantastic legs were bare, her feet tucked into pink sandals. He couldn't see her eyes because of her sunglasses, but he felt her gaze all the way to his soul.

Ashley felt her heart slam against her ribs when Justin stepped out onto the porch clad only in low-riding jeans. Her secret hope that he would be glad to see her bit the dust in a hurry. He looked less than pleased by her impromptu arrival. His eyes were a cool blue and there was no warmth in the hard line of his mouth. That, added to the dark shadow covering his jaw and chin, gave him a dimension of danger. She swallowed, wishing she'd called first.

"Such an unexpected pleasure."

The blatant sarcasm lacing his words stung, but Ashley refused to let it show. "Can I talk to you?" she asked.

He leaned a shoulder against the railing and crossed his arms over his chest. "As a rule I refuse to speak to anyone who shows up without an invitation. But for you I'll make an exception."

She stared at him wondering what had possessed her to come here. She'd been wrong, hoping there was a way to go back and fix things between them. Anything he'd felt for her had obviously been destroyed when she'd walked away with Geoffrey.

"You know, Ashley, my time is pretty expensive these days," he chided. "If you've got something to say, be quick about it."

She was thankful for her sunglasses, thankful he couldn't see the tears burning her eyes. She shook her head and took a step back. "Never mind. I guess there's nothing to say after all."

"It's easier to run, isn't it? No risk involved in that." The intensity of his gaze challenged her. "For once, why don't you take an uncalculated chance and tell me why you're here."

"I came to ask for your help," she admitted stiffly.

His eyes narrowed. "My help? How could I possibly help you now?"

"I'm having some trouble wading through all the offers and things." She moistened her lips nervously. "I thought you might be able to help me sort things out." When he didn't immediately respond, she blurted, "I'll pay you."

"Pay me?" The words burst from him, his tone coated with disgust. "I offered to help you at the beginning and you didn't take it. Why are you willing to pay for it now?"

She shrugged helplessly. "Things have turned out a lot more complicated than I anticipated."

"Have they? I think I may have mentioned that was a possibility."

She felt a spark of anger. It felt good compared to the numbness she'd been experiencing. "A simple yes or no will do, Justin."

"What happened to your fiancé? Why can't he take care of things for you?"

"It's really none of your business, but Geoffrey and I are no longer together."

"Why doesn't that surprise me?" Justin murmured. "Tell me something. Was he trying to spend your money too fast, or did you realize with that kind of money you didn't need your true love after all?"

Her temper snapped. She whirled away from him and started toward her car. "Go to hell, Justin," she tossed over her shoulder. "Forget I was ever here."

With her back turned, she never saw him move. She never knew he'd come down off the porch until his hand clamped around her upper arm and he roughly swung her around to face him. He whipped the glasses from her face and tossed them to the ground.

"I've tried every day for the last six weeks to forget you were ever here," he ground out. "As a matter of fact, I haven't had an easy moment since you climbed out of your car at the marina. The very last thing I need is you waltzing in and out of my life at your convenience. You made it

clear when you left here that I had nothing good enough
to offer you. So I have to wonder exactly what it is you're
looking for now."

She looked into his face, shaken by the intensity of his
anger, by the depth of his bitterness. His fingers bit into her
tender flesh, but that pain was merely a twinge compared to
the shattering of her heart.

"I thought you might be able to help me," she said
flatly. "I'm sorry I bothered you."

He continued to glare at her, his eyes sizzling with temper. Finally, he released her and stepped back. "I'll help
you, but not because you asked. I'll do it because this whole
thing started as a favor to Nick. I'll finish it for the same
reason. Understand?"

She nodded, not trusting herself to speak.

"Where are you staying?"

"At Jessi's."

"Fine. I'll be over this evening around eight and we'll
go over everything you have." He turned and started back
to the porch. "Be ready, Ashley. We won't drag this out
any longer than necessary."

She watched as he disappeared inside the house without
a backward glance. Absently, she rubbed her arm where
his fingers had left an uncomfortable tingling. She'd been
a fool to come, hoping there might be a chance she could
still mean something to him. He'd just made it perfectly
clear that he wanted nothing more to do with her than
was absolutely necessary. She'd been hoping for a second
chance. He was offering her none.

Chapter Ten

Feeling tense and edgy, Ashley sat across from Justin at Jessi's dining room table. Spread before him were letters she'd received and telephone messages she'd taken. One by one he sorted through them. He hadn't spoken for at least twenty minutes, and Ashley let the silence stand.

When he'd arrived at the house, all traces of the angry man she'd encountered that morning had been carefully concealed. She was sure that to Cal and Jessi he looked the same as usual. He'd acted the same, exchanging teasing remarks and flirting with Angie and Jessi. Only Ashley knew that behind the friendly mask was a man who couldn't wait to get her out of his life for good.

"You've got some interesting offers here," he said without looking up. "Do you want to do them all?"

"I don't know. What do you think?"

He glanced at her briefly. "It doesn't matter what I think. You have to make the decisions."

"But I don't know what I'm deciding on. I'm asking for your advice. What's involved if I accept any of those offers? I need you to help me understand."

He regarded her a long moment, something unreadable moving through his eyes. Finally, he looked away and began to gather the stacks of paper together. "Okay. This is what we'll do. I'll make some phone calls and get all the details. Then you can make your decisions. One thing I'm sure of is that you'll have to do some traveling."

"Will you go with me?"

His head snapped up at that. "What the hell do you want? A full-time baby-sitter?"

"No." She met his gaze straight on, determined not to be daunted by his quick show of anger. "I want someone I can trust."

The impact of her words were instantly visible before he swiftly concealed his surprise. She watched as he slid the papers into a manila folder and then pushed his chair back to stand. When his eyes met hers again, there was absolutely no hint of his feelings revealed there.

His smile was cold as he picked up the folder. "If that's the case, then I'm not the man you want. You made that perfectly clear a few weeks ago." He turned and was out of the room before she could react to the harsh words.

Leaning forward, she rested her elbows on the table and covered her face with her hands. She was so tired and discouraged. It had taken her two weeks to work up enough courage to come here to face him. Somehow she'd convinced herself that he'd be more forgiving, more approachable. But now she might as well face the truth and save herself further heartache. There was no reaching him. He was a stranger to her, and she couldn't very well tell a stranger that she'd fallen in love with him.

She would have laughed at that thought if she hadn't been so afraid she'd start crying and never stop. Two months ago she never would have believed she would ever face this kind of dilemma. She'd had her life planned out so carefully. Everything had been so neat and tidy, with no room allotted for messy emotions to come into play and wreak havoc on her organized life.

A light touch on her shoulder had her lowering her hands. Angie studied her with wide green eyes filled with a child's compassion. It was more than Ashley could bear. Tears gathered in her eyes and traced down her cheeks.

Angie reached up and Ashley gathered the child onto

her lap. Slender arms wrapped around her neck and little voice whispered close to her ear, "Don't cry, Ashley. It'll be okay."

The comforting words offered by a three-year-old only made Ashley cry harder.

"Ashley, I forgot to ask you about—" Justin stopped in the doorway, startled by the scene before him.

Angie turned concerned eyes to him, her head still resting against Ashley's shoulder. "Ashley's sad," she said solemnly. "You can make her happy, Justin. Can't you?"

Justin felt as if his stomach dropped to the vicinity of his knees. He knew he was a hero in Angie's eyes, able to do anything. But he didn't feel much like a hero now. He felt like a man caught in a situation he was handling very poorly.

He walked over and laid the file folder on the table before lifting Angie into his arms. Ashley quickly rose and moved to the window, her back to him as she surreptitiously wiped at the tears on her cheeks.

"You run along," he told Angie. "I need to talk to Ashley."

Angie looked into his face. "Will you make her feel better?"

"I don't know."

"I didn't make her feel better. I think I made her cry more."

Justin sighed and kissed her cheek. He carried her to the door, then set her on her feet. Her bare toes peeked out from the edge of her pink nightgown. "You didn't make her cry more," he assured her as he crouched down to her level. "Sometimes there's nothing you can say to make someone feel better. Sometimes they just need to cry."

Angie chewed on her bottom lip thoughtfully. "But you'll try to make her feel better, won't you, Justin?"

"Yeah. I'll try."

"Good." Angie cast one last look in Ashley's direction before turning to leave the room.

Justin rose and slowly crossed to where Ashley stood at the window. He had no idea what to say to her.

He'd been battling his own churning emotions since her unexpected arrival. Every day since her departure, he'd imagined what it would be like if she returned. He'd had this misty vision of her coming back because she'd realized she loved him. In reality, it hurt to know she was here only because she needed his help. In response to that, he'd used his anger to build a wall of animosity between them, when all he really wanted was to touch her, hold her, kiss her.

All he really wanted was a chance to convince her that loving him wasn't such a terrible risk.

"Leave me alone, Justin," she said, her voice barely above a whisper.

"Why are you crying?"

"You wouldn't understand."

"I want to."

"No, you don't. Just go away."

"Ashley." Gently he caught her elbow and urged her to face him. "I don't like seeing you like this."

"I know." She drew in a deep, ragged breath and pulled her arm free. "You've made it crystal clear that you don't like seeing me at all." Tears glistened on her cheeks and pooled in her dark eyes.

"I—"

"No, don't," she cut in. "There's nothing left to say." With that she moved around him and hurried from the room.

Justin was staring at an empty doorway when Cal stepped into it. "That's one unhappy lady," he observed.

"No kidding." Justin slid his hands into his jeans pockets and shook his head. "And I was supposed to cheer her up."

"Your technique needs some improvement."

Justin gave a cynical laugh. "I need a technique."

"What did you do to Ashley?" Jessi demanded as she marched into the room. She didn't stop until she stood directly in front of Justin, effectively laying the blame at his feet. "She's really upset."

"I know."

Her green eyes widened. "So? What did you do?"

Justin rubbed his forehead. "I think it's more a question of what I didn't do."

"I encouraged her to come to you for help. I thought after the way things turned out between you two, that you'd welcome a second chance to work things out."

"I told you not to meddle," Cal stated.

Jessi turned to him, hands planted firmly on her hips. "I'm not meddling," she denied hotly. "It was obvious Justin was upset when Ashley left. It was just as obvious that Ashley was struggling to deal with all the stuff that came along after catching that silly fish. It looked like a perfect opportunity for them to get back together and maybe work things out. That's not meddling. That's helping people you care about."

"You make it sound logical, but it's still meddling. And now look what you've caused."

"That's not fair! You're just—"

"Time out!" Justin raised his voice above the din and brought his hands together in the official referee signal. "I've got enough trouble without adding you two to my growing list. Okay?"

A stony silence descended upon the room. Jessi folded her arms tightly against her chest and stared down at the floor. Cal assumed exactly the same stance only he was staring at the ceiling.

"Come on, you guys," Justin cajoled. "Kiss and make up. I can't handle the pressure of knowing your marriage folded because of me."

"Yeah, right," Cal scoffed. "As if I'd let the likes of you come between me and my bride of seven years."

"Eight, almost nine," Jessi corrected with a sigh. "Lord, Cal, can't you ever get it right?"

He grinned sheepishly. "Being married to you is such a joy that I just lose track of the time."

The stern expression on her face melted away as she laughed softly. "You're hopeless."

"Hopelessly in love with you." He closed the distance between them and caught her close.

"You're real smooth, too."

"You bet." He bent and she tilted her head back. The kiss was a meeting in the middle.

Justin watched, both amused and envious. They made it look so easy, and he knew better. Marriage was hard work. He'd never considered it a job he wanted until Ashley had walked into his life. When she'd walked out and driven off with Anderson, he'd known he'd never consider it again.

He'd consciously made the decision not to pursue her once she returned to Knoxville, knowing if they stood any chance at all of building a lasting relationship, she would have to be the one to make the first move. Well, it appeared she was doing just that. Unfortunately, he'd been so busy nursing his wounded ego, he'd nearly missed it. It didn't matter what reason she gave for coming back. It mattered that she was here. He had a lot of backtracking to do to set things right.

He cleared his throat discreetly and waited for the lingering kiss to end.

Cal finally lifted his head and shot him a mischievous look. "You still here?"

"Afraid so."

Jessi turned, her cheeks flushed with color. "You see, Justin, a little conflict is good for a relationship. It's a lot of fun to make up. You might want to try it with Ashley."

"I don't think now would be a good time." He picked up the folder and prepared to leave. "I think I'll wait until tomorrow. Start everything all over again."

Jessi frowned. "I didn't do the wrong thing, did I?"

"Don't worry about it. Ashley caught me off guard, that's all. We'll work it out."

"I think she really cares about you. And I think she's really surprised by her feelings."

Knowing Ashley, any feelings she might have for him had to come as an absolute shock. The fact that she came back said a lot about those feelings. It took courage for her to do it. And so far he'd done everything in his power to make her regret her decision.

He bid Cal and Jessi good night and slipped out into

the warm summer night. Stars littered the night sky, surrounding a lopsided moon.

Justin cut across the yard and headed for the Blazer. When he started to open the door, a strange sensation washed over him. He paused and looked up at the dark window on the end of the house. He couldn't see her, but he knew Ashley stood within the shadows of the guest room, watching.

He almost went back inside, an overwhelming urge to set things right between them blindsiding him. It suddenly seemed imperative that he apologize for the way he'd treated her today. Then he hesitated, trying to decide what was best for her. She was upset now, hurt by his harsh words. Perhaps it would be better to wait until tomorrow when she was calmer and he'd had a chance to order his thoughts.

Tomorrow would be better, he decided as he reached to open the truck door. Tomorrow they could start fresh. A new beginning.

Ashley saw Justin pause and look toward her window. The lights were off in the room and she knew he couldn't see her. Still, she felt his gaze as surely as a touch. He knew she was there watching. She wished she knew what his thoughts were.

Sighing heavily, she turned away and went to sit on the edge of the bed. Nothing was going the way she had hoped. He was so angry, and she didn't know how to make him understand. She nearly laughed at that, realizing that she barely understood. How could she expect Justin to have a clue?

She stood and turned on the light at the same instant a soft knock came at the door. She opened it to find Jessi there.

After a quick appraisal, Jessi announced, "I know just what you need."

Ashley gave a hesitant smile, wondering at the mischief she saw in her friend's eyes. "What might that be?"

"Chocolate." She grinned. "Angie is in bed, and Cal's

got his nose stuck in a book. Let's you and me slip into Windsong and hit the Dairy Bar. They have a great double chocolate ice cream cone. It's the best in the world."

"Sounds better than men right now."

"Well, I don't know about that, but it's close."

Ashley chuckled. "Give me a minute."

"I'll meet you downstairs."

Ashley exchanged her sandals for a pair of canvas shoes and checked her reflection in the mirror. She grimaced, hating the way the tears had reddened her nose and eyes. It was all Justin's fault, she decided as she tried to repair the damage with a touch of makeup. If he would just bend a little instead of being so inflexible. Maybe then she could tell him how she really felt.

She sighed and stared through her reflection. The fact of the matter was she'd hurt him when she'd left, and he didn't seem inclined to give her another shot. She couldn't really blame him. Maybe it would be best if they didn't attempt to go back and pick up the pieces of the fragile relationship that had developed between them. Justin had certainly made his choice clear.

She felt despair begin to rise inside and clamped down on it. Now was not the time to make any kind of decision. Her emotions were running too close to the surface. She needed some time to sort things out.

Determined to push everything out of her mind for a little while, she turned and picked up her purse. A double chocolate ice cream cone sounded like the perfect solution right now.

Ashley sat on the Miles's front porch, idly rocking away the lazy summer afternoon. Cal had gone into town following lunch, and Jessi was downstairs working on her Family Folks while Angie napped.

Considering how little she'd slept last night, Ashley knew a nap might do her some good, too. But she was still tense from yesterday's confrontation with Justin and didn't think sleep would be any easier now than it had been during the night. So she'd opted for a wicker rocker on the front porch, hoping the tranquil atmosphere would help calm her nerves.

It seemed to be working until she spotted Justin's Blazer round the curve and turn into the long gravel driveway. Billowing dust drifted away on the breeze as he parked behind her car.

Ashley forced herself to stay put on the porch, but she couldn't control the acceleration of her pulse as she watched Justin climb out of his truck and saunter toward the porch. As usual, he wore snug jeans with a dark blue tee shirt tucked in at the waist. In his hand was the file folder he'd taken home last night.

"You do a great imitation of a true Southern belle," he said as he climbed the steps. "All you need is a fan."

The warm timbre of his voice coupled with that trademark sexy grin had her heart turning somersaults. This was the man she'd come back to see. This was the man she'd fallen in love with.

"I *am* a true Southern belle, born and raised here," she reminded him. "You're the imposter."

His smiled faded as he nodded. "In a lot of ways." He continued to regard her with those enigmatic eyes, causing her breath to back up in her lungs. It was crazy the things this man did to her. Crazy and wonderful and awful. It had to be love, because nothing else made sense.

"I may not be a true Southern gentleman," he said softly, "but I'm enough of a man to know when I owe a lady an apology. I'm sorry for the way I treated you yesterday, Ashley. You caught me by surprise and I was way out of line."

Relief rippled through her, followed by a renewed burst of hope. Maybe it wasn't too late after all. "Apology accepted."

"Thank you." He flashed another of those breathtaking smiles before making himself comfortable on the top step and opening the folder. "I've been busy on the phone this morning. Want to hear what I found out?"

She listened as he gave a brief synopsis of the various phone calls he'd made and the options open to her. Once he'd finished, he closed the folder and handed it to her.

"I've made some notes in there. If you've got any questions, just ask. I'll be glad to call everyone when you decide what you want to do."

"Thank you," she said, taking the folder. "I appreciate your help, Justin."

"No problem." He scooted back to rest against the railing and stretched out his legs. "Where is everyone today?"

"Cal went into town. Angie is napping and Jessi is working downstairs."

"And you're taking it easy on the porch."

"I'm actually getting pretty good at leisure activities."

He smiled. "Are you ready for your trip to the Big Apple next week?"

"As ready as I'll ever be." She shrugged. "I'll be glad when the whole thing is over. Enough is enough already."

"I know what you mean."

"Has it been bad for you around here since everyone found out who you are?"

He shook his head. "Not really. There've been a few disparaging remarks, but nothing to get excited about. I've pretty much ignored the whole thing. I think folks are starting to take my cue and do the same. I'll know things are back to normal when Bea Jenkins starts telling me dirty jokes again."

Ashley laughed. "That's your barometer, huh?"

"It's been awful having her call me Mr. Holmes." He gave a mock shudder. "I keep looking over my shoulder, expecting my father to be standing there."

"Has all this media attention affected your family?"

"It caught them by surprise. My mother read me the riot act for not filling them in on the details before the first reporter cornered them." He shrugged. "She's right. I should have let them know so they could have prepared for the deluge."

"Have you talked to your father?"

"No." He drew a deep breath and let it out slowly. "But I've decided I'm going to see him next week when I'm in New York."

Surprise jolted her. "I . . . I didn't know you were planning to go."

"I thought I'd make an appearance. A brief one."

"Good. And it's good that you're going to see your father."

He gave a wry chuckle. "Well, we'll see about that. He may toss me out the window of his high-rise office and we'll make headlines again."

Ashley shook her head. "No, he won't. He'll be glad to see you."

"Maybe." Justin glanced at his watch and stood. "I need to get going. I'm meeting a group of doctors at the marina in a half hour. They'll be staying at the cabin the next three days." He started down the steps and she stood and crossed the porch. He turned and looked up at her. "I guess I'll see you in New York then."

"I guess so."

He raked a hand through his hair and looked away from her. If she hadn't known better, she would have thought he was nervous about something. But that made no sense at all. She couldn't remember Justin ever being nervous about anything.

"You know," he said suddenly, "I give a pretty good tour of the Big Apple. If you've got time while you're there, maybe we could do some sightseeing together."

She smiled, finding this slightly uncertain Justin as endearing as the take-charge man she was used to. "That sounds like fun. I'll look forward to it."

"Good." He nodded as he backed away. Then he stopped, fixed her with a narrow-eyed look before starting back toward the porch. Before she had time to blink, his hands gripped her waist and he lowered her to the ground. Her hands had gone instinctively to his shoulders, and she left them there while they stood in the summer sunshine staring at one another.

"I can't leave here without telling you I'm glad you came back," he said, his voice pitched low. "And I'm glad you don't hold a grudge when a man acts like an idiot."

"Well, I know a little bit about acting like an idiot. Sometimes it just happens without any good reason."

His hands tightened on her waist, drew her a fraction of an inch closer. "Can I kiss you goodbye?"

She shook her head. "Why don't you kiss me hello instead?"

"Hello," he whispered just before his lips covered hers for an achingly tender kiss.

Ashley slid her arms around his neck, and despite the fierce pounding of her heart, felt a wonderful serenity wrap around her. All the lingering doubts she'd been struggling with melted under the heat of his kiss. She loved Justin Holmes with a certainty she still didn't quite understand, but didn't have any desire to question. Nothing in her life had ever felt as right as this. And she intended to be recklessly spontaneous and tell him so as soon as he allowed her to catch her breath again.

"Mama, come quick!"

The excited, childish squeal caused Ashley and Justin to spring apart like two guilty adolescents.

"Justin is kissing Ashley again!" Angie announced in a voice loud enough to inform half the county.

Ashley felt her cheeks heat as Jessi appeared at the screen door behind her daughter. Her gaze shifted from Ashley to Justin and back again before a big grin appeared.

"I can't leave you two alone for a minute," she scolded.

"Busted again," Justin admitted with a laugh. He winked at Ashley before going to the porch to give Angie a quick hug. "I've got to get going. I'm late."

With a strange mixture of elation and disappointment, Ashley watched as he jogged to his truck. Once he'd driven out of sight, she turned and climbed the steps.

Jessi was waiting there, a knowing smile on her face. "Bad timing, I guess."

"It's okay. He's going to be in New York next week, too. We'll have time to talk then."

And neither of us is leaving that city until I've told him exactly how I feel, she vowed silently.

For eight years Justin had avoided coming to New York City in the summer. Heat rose up from the concrete, and humidity hung like a physical cloud over the city, obscuring the tops of the skyscrapers. All along the streets of Manhattan people and traffic rushed in every direction. In that respect the city had not changed in the time he'd been gone. He realized with a satisfying certainty that he hadn't missed any of the craziness.

His view of the city from twenty stories up was a testament of man's powerful ability to create his own environment. With the exception of the sky and a few trees that somehow managed to grow despite the abundance of concrete, there was nothing natural in sight. Buildings stretched to the horizon, the taller ones overshadowing the smaller. It was an awesome view, but not one he wanted to wake to every day of his life.

Turning back into the lush suite provided by Still Waters, he glanced again at his watch, noting that it was only ten minutes later than the last time he'd checked.

When he'd arrived at the hotel at four, he'd stowed his luggage in his room and had gone directly to Ashley's room. He'd been surprised and disappointed when she hadn't answered his knock. They'd talked on the phone last night and she'd known what time he expected to be there.

Now at half past five he told himself not to worry. Something had probably come up that she needed to take care of. After all, she wasn't obligated to be there for him. When she returned to her room and got his message, he was sure she'd call. At least he hoped so.

Still, he was anxious to see her. He kept reliving that searing kiss they'd shared in the Miles's front yard. There had been nothing tentative about her response. And in the heartbeat before his lips claimed hers, he'd seen a promising light in her eyes that made him think of everlasting love.

A knock on his door brought an instant sense of relief and an expectant smile to his face. He crossed the room swiftly and opened the door, fully intending to pull Ashley into his arms. He wasn't prepared to do the same with the uniformed bellhop who stood there, an apologetic smile on his young face.

"I'm sorry, Mr. Holmes, but this message should have been given to you when you arrived." He extended his hand, a small white envelope clasped in his fingers. "The desk clerk overlooked it."

"Thank you." Justin took the piece of stationery and offered a tip. Without further comment he closed the door and ripped open the envelope. He unfolded the single sheet of paper to reveal Ashley's neat handwriting. Her message was brief. *I owe you a dinner. Tonight—7:00—The Emerald Room. See you then.*

He reread the words three times before a relieved chuckle moved through him. Some intuition told him this just might be a night he'd never forget.

Chapter Eleven

The room appeared to be empty. Spotless white damask cloths covered tables void of place settings. Imported silk of emerald and ecru cascaded down the walls. The carpeting, a rich emerald, navy, and rose blend stretched from wall-to-wall, except for the small parquet dance floor at the far end of the long room. The soft instrumental music drifting on the air and the lighting were low, intimate, seductive.

Ashley sat at a table in the back, away from the kitchen and nearly out of sight of the entrance. A single white rose in an emerald crystal bud vase sat at her elbow with a tall candle glowing beside it. The silver was sterling, the china Wedgwood, and the stemware Baccarat. On the table next to hers, an excellent vintage champagne chilled.

The mood was definitely set. Now all she needed was Justin.

A tremor of apprehension shot through her before she could control it. She had never in her entire life intentionally set out to entice a man. And she was going to feel very foolish if the man in question didn't show up for the event.

She glanced at the slim watch on her wrist, saw that it was just after seven and felt a quick stab of anxiety. What if he didn't come? What if he was upset with her for not meeting him this afternoon? What if he didn't get her note?

Ruthlessly, she clamped down on the rising panic. If she had a hope of pulling this evening off, she needed to get hold of herself now.

Lifting her anxious gaze to the door, she suddenly felt everything slip away. He was there in the shadows, standing just inside the room. Dressed entirely in black from the open collar of his soft dress shirt to the soles of his shoes, she wondered if her mind had managed to magically conjure his image. But there was nothing imaginary about the man moving toward her.

He stopped behind the chair across from her, and she tipped her head back to look up at him. She wasn't sure she was breathing, wasn't really sure it was a necessary function right now. She was captured by blue eyes and the promise she saw there. It was enough to make her believe in love and romance and happily ever after endings.

"I'm glad you could join me," she said, her voice sounding just a bit on the breathless side.

"I almost never turn down a free meal." He pulled the chair out and sat down. "Especially when the invitation is issued by a beautiful lady."

"Thank you."

Justin gazed at her realizing he was seeing yet another fascinating side of her. Tonight her hair was swept up in a smooth chignon that managed to look both sophisticated and touchable. Already he was hoping for the opportunity to mess it up later. He wasn't exactly sure what she wore, but what he could see was bright and brief. The turquoise fabric draped softly around her neck, leaving her shoulders bare and dipping into a tantalizing, lacy vee in the front. It was one of those little numbers designed to capture a man's attention and keep it. Something told him the lower half of the outfit was probably as interesting as the top.

With his blood pressure on the rise, he forced himself to look away from her and around the room. "Is there a reason why we seem to have one of the hotel's best restaurants all to ourselves?"

The sound of her warm, husky laugh stroked like velvet fingers down his back. He turned his attention back to her to see humor sparkling in her eyes. But he saw something more there. Something dark and edgy, and just a little uncertain.

"It's amazing what a little money will buy," she murmured. "For a fee we are able to enjoy all this elegance, along with a wonderful meal, and not have to share it with anyone."

"For a woman who doesn't believe in romance, you've done a fantastic job of setting the perfect romantic evening for two."

"Don't you know I've been converted, Justin?"

"Have you?" He reached across the table to cover her hand with his own. Automatically she linked her fingers with his, the movement easy and natural. His gaze dropped to their joined hands and he realized all over again that she was everything he'd ever need or want. They fit together. He wondered if she felt it too.

When he looked up, he no longer had to wonder. She smiled at him, her eyes warmed by a love so deep and clear it momentarily startled him.

"Dance with me," she invited.

"I'd love to." He released her hand and stood. "I'm dying to see what the rest of that outfit looks like."

"Well, hang on."

Before he could question her warning, she was on her feet, and he understood. His mouth went dry and his pulse scrambled before finding a steady, though slightly elevated rhythm. His response was immediate and strictly male. A man didn't look at a woman dressed like that and wonder what she thought about current world affairs. A man looked at a woman dressed like that and wondered what she could possibly be wearing beneath the slinky fabric.

While the brief turquoise top loosely skimmed her body, the skirt clung like a second skin. The wild print of turquoise and black was short enough to reveal a tantalizing length of shapely legs adorned in sheer black stockings. A black silk scarf was tied at her waist as a belt, and shiny black heels brought her nearly eye level with him. He took his time, running his gaze from top to bottom in a thorough inspection.

"What do you think?" Ashley asked playfully. "I bought it this afternoon in a little shop on Fifth Avenue. The saleswoman guaranteed me it would knock the socks off any red-blooded man. I bought it with you in mind."

"Thank you and my socks are long gone."

She laughed, her cheeks flushed. He reached for her hand and led her to the dance floor. An instrumental version of a popular Neil Diamond ballad floated on the air. Justin drew her close and set an easy pace, even though he was just about ready to jump out of his skin.

All of his senses hummed at a heightened level. He stroked his hand down her bare back, her skin like silk beneath his fingers. The tantalizing brush of her breasts against his chest sent shock waves of sensation through him, while her usual light scent teased him. And the feel of her hands resting just above his belt made him think of more intimate caresses.

She drew back to look at him, a teasing glint in her dark eyes. "You seem a little tense. Are you okay?"

He considered her a long, thorough moment. "You wouldn't be trying to seduce me, would you, Ashley?"

"Maybe." She shifted, reaching up to rest her arms on his shoulders. Her body brushed his with just enough heat to set him on fire. "If I were, how would I be doing?"

"I'd say that the job is nearly done. And that you might want to be careful from this point on."

She shook her head. "I'm not afraid of you, Justin. Not anymore."

The music ended, and together they walked back to the table. Justin nodded toward the chilling champagne. "Were you planning to ply me with that stuff until I lost my head?"

"If necessary."

"It's not. But let's have some anyway."

He poured a glass and handed it to her, then poured one for himself. He stared a moment at the effervescent bubbles before shifting his gaze to Ashley. "Shall we propose a toast?"

She lifted her glass by the delicate stem and extended it toward him. "To us," she whispered.

Tilting his glass, he touched it to hers. "To us."

Her gaze never wavered as she drank and then set her glass aside. He did the same, acutely aware of the intensity in her eyes and the crackle of awareness in the air.

She stepped closer, her hand came up to touch his cheek. "I love you, Justin."

The simple announcement staggered him. The words, spoken strong and clear, left no room for doubt. In his heart he'd known, but it still hadn't prepared him for hearing them spoken so sincerely.

She urged his head downward and he tasted both champagne and heat on her lips. Desire roared through his bloodstream like molten lava. His hands made a hurried sweep of her bare back from shoulder to waist before urging her closer. She wrapped her arms around his neck and let her body melt into his. And that was all it took to transform flickering embers of passion into a full-blown blaze.

Justin wanted to walk directly into the heart of the fire and stay there until he'd had his fill of her. He doubted that a lifetime would be long enough. She tasted of dark pleasure, but her body pressed to his promised sweet heaven.

He drew back from her slightly, watching as her eyes opened and focused on his. A provocative smile curved her mouth, and he felt hot longing slash through him. He ran a thumb along her jaw line in a light caress.

"I love you."

She laughed lightly. "I know."

"I want to make love to you," he murmured. "Over and over again. All night long."

"Here?"

He saw mischief dancing with desire in her eyes. She'd never been more beautiful. "I thought my room might be a little more comfortable."

"Now I think you're trying to seduce me."

"Yeah? How am I doing?"

She stepped out of his arms and took his hand. "Why don't we go to your room and find out."

He held back a moment, looking at the beautiful table and half-full glasses of champagne. "What about your romantic dinner?"

She tugged him toward the door. "Don't worry about it. We'll have it delivered to your room when we're ready for it."

"Covered all the bases, huh?"

"Actually, I'm just going with the flow." Her laughter flowed over him like warm honey as they stepped into the elevator. "It's another new personality trait I'm trying to develop."

She turned to him as the doors slid soundlessly shut. Her arms slipped around his waist and instantly she had him wrapped in a sensual haze filled only with her. Her scent surrounded him. Her touch tempted him. Her very essence claimed him—mind, body, and soul.

He had no idea how they made it from the elevator to his room. When his brain finally managed to focus again, Ashley was busy releasing the buttons on his shirt. The room was softly lit by the city nightlife shining through the windows. It was just enough light for him to see what a treasure he'd found in this particular woman. He still wasn't sure how he'd arrived at this point in his life. He hadn't been looking for love. But now that he'd found it, now that she'd given it to him, he knew he had everything he'd ever need.

She smiled up at him as her hands tugged his shirttail free and pushed the garment off his arms. Carelessly, she let it drop to the floor. Her hands smoothed over his shoulders before gliding downward through the hair covering his chest. "I want to touch you," she whispered.

He gave an unsteady laugh. "Well, I'm not going to try to stop you."

"Good." Her hands worked the buckle of his belt "I want all of you this time. If you're not prepared, I am."

"A practical woman." His breath caught as she pushed his trousers down over his hips. They pooled at his feet, and he stepped out of them and his shoes.

She made a sound deep in her throat as she let her hands skim his body. "The socks need to go," she decided as she knelt before him.

Justin couldn't have formed a reply if his life had depended on it. Hell, he'd thought she'd knocked his socks off back in the restaurant. As she peeled off first one and then the other, her hair brushed his thigh, setting off a knee-weakening response. He didn't know what was keeping him on his feet. Maybe just anticipation of what she would do next.

He wasn't disappointed. As she straightened, she ran her hands up his legs until they were resting on the waistband of his briefs. She leaned into him and pressed her lips against his neck, sending ripples of desire coursing through him.

Ashley could feel his pulse hammering beneath her lips and marveled a moment at the fact that his heart beat for her. She felt fingers in her hair and waited while he pulled each pin free. The simple task sent chills skittering over her skin. When he removed the last one, he combed his fingers through the stands until they fell freely to her shoulders.

She looked up into his face and felt her breath back up in her throat. His eyes were bright, electric with emotion so pure and sweet it left her weak. Had she really been willing to go through life without experiencing the delight that came when he looked at her just this way?

"I want forever, Ashley. Thick and thin. Better or worse. The whole nine yards."

She felt tears sting her eyes as pure joy bubbled wildly inside. "You got it," she promised.

He gave her a quick, hard kiss, then said, "Now, I think under the circumstances, you're overdressed."

"Not for long." She took a step back as she untied the scarf at her waist and let it drift to the floor. Next, she reached up behind her neck and released the one catch there. The silky dress parted and pooled briefly at her waist before she shimmied out of it completely. She was left in nothing more than sheer black panty hose.

"Very economical," he commented with a slow smile.

"Two step process." She started to peel the hose off, but his hands closed over hers.

"Don't." His voice was husky. "My treat. I have a thing for nylon. Especially when it's covering those legs." His hand smoothed down over her hip to her thigh before trailing back up to cup her breast.

"I'll keep that in mind for future reference," she whispered just before her whole thought process closed down and sensation became the ruling factor.

As before, he carried her away swiftly and surely. The bed became a soft haven beneath them as he worked his magic. He touched and tasted and teased. And she learned. She learned that in this shimmering world of delight, she could return the pleasure to him in much the same way she received it.

And when he came to her fully, the greatest mysteries of all were revealed. The beauty of two hearts beating as one. The strength of one love as durable as humankind. The gift of life as old as time.

Even at three A.M., New York City still glistened and hummed with activity. The Big Apple never slept. And on this particular night, neither did Ashley and Justin.

It had been nearly ten when Ashley had called and had dinner brought to the room. She and Justin had enjoyed a fantastic meal, then gone back to bed for an entirely different feast. Now they sat together in a deep armchair and gazed out at the sleepless city. She was wrapped in a sheet and nestled securely in his arms, her head resting on his shoulder.

He pressed a kissed to her forehead. "I'll never look at this city again without thinking of this night," he murmured. "Thank you for a wonderful memory."

"My pleasure." She nearly purred with contentment. "I never dreamed I could be this happy."

"And to think not so long ago you were such a cynic."

She tilted her head back to look up at him. "I guess all I needed was the love of a good man."

"That you've got." He paused for a lingering kiss. When

he lifted his head, he said softly, "Will you marry me, Miss Harper?"

"Yes," she answered without the slightest hesitation.

He grinned. "When?"

She shifted on his lap so that she could wind her arms around his neck. "Name the time and place and I'll be there."

He shook his head. "This is your call. I want you to have the kind of wedding you want."

"Okay." She studied him a long moment, loving him even more for his consideration. "When I thought I was going to marry Geoffrey, I wanted a big wedding with all the trimmings. But I don't care about any of that now. All I want now is me and you, and your family, including J.T., and my family and Jessi and Cal and Angie." She smiled. "Something simple and beautiful. Like our love."

"Sounds perfect."

His fingers caressed her cheek as he dipped his head and found her lips with his own. She tightened her arms around his neck and let herself sink into the kiss and the promise of a future filled with happiness.

About the Author

Patricia Lynn has loved reading and writing since grade school. In her teens, she wrote her stories in longhand and gave them to her friends to read. In 1993, with her family's support, she finally decided to pursue full-time her dream of becoming a published author. Her one wish is that people enjoy reading her books as much as she enjoys writing them. Patricia loves hearing from readers and can be reached at P.O. Box 47427, Indianapolis, IN 46247.